LUCKY
Shot

by

USA Today Bestselling Author
SHANNA HATFIELD

Book 9

A Sweet Western Romance

Lucky Shot
Pink Pistol Sisterhood, Book 9

Copyright ©2023 by Shanna Hatfield

ISBN: 9798397152013

All rights reserved. No part of this publication may be reproduced, distributed, downloaded, decompiled, reverse engineered, transmitted, or stored in or introduced into any information storage and retrieval system, in any form or by any means, including photocopying, recording, or other electronic or mechanical methods, now known or hereafter invented, without the written permission of the author, except in the case of brief quotations embodied in reviews and certain other noncommercial uses permitted by copyright law. Please purchase only authorized editions.

For permission requests, please contact the author, with a subject line of "permission request" at the email address below or through her website.

Shanna Hatfield
shanna@shannahatfield.com

This is a work of fiction. Names, characters, businesses, places, events, and incidents either are the product of the author's imagination or are used in a fictitious manner. Any resemblance to actual persons, living or dead, business establishments, or actual events is purely coincidental.

Published by Wholesome Hearts Publishing, LLC.
wholesomeheartspublishing@gmail.com

*To my dad –
for all the great memories I have
of our adventures in ol' Orange,
&
to my Pink Pistol Sisters
for all the wonderful ideas
that brought the Summer of 1972 to life!*

Books by Shanna Hatfield

FICTION

CONTEMPORARY

Holiday Brides
Valentine Bride
Summer Bride
Easter Bride
Lilac Bride
Lake Bride

Rodeo Romance
The Christmas Cowboy
Wrestling Christmas
Capturing Christmas
Barreling Through Christmas
Chasing Christmas
Racing Christmas
Keeping Christmas
Roping Christmas
Remembering Christmas
Savoring Christmas

Grass Valley Cowboys
The Cowboy's Christmas Plan
The Cowboy's Spring Romance
The Cowboy's Summer Love
The Cowboy's Autumn Fall
The Cowboy's New Heart
The Cowboy's Last Goodbye

Summer Creek
Catching the Cowboy
Rescuing the Rancher
Protecting the Princess
Distracting the Deputy
Guiding the Grouch

Women of Tenacity
Heart of Clay
Heart of Hope
Heart of Love

HISTORICAL

Pendleton Petticoats
Dacey   Bertie
Aundy   Millie
Caterina   Dally
Ilsa   Quinn
Marnie   Evie
Lacey   Sadie

Baker City Brides
Crumpets and Cowpies
Thimbles and Thistles
Corsets and Cuffs
Bobbins and Boots
Lightning and Lawmen
Dumplings and Dynamite

Hearts of the War
Garden of Her Heart
Home of Her Heart
Dream of Her Heart

Hardman Holidays
The Christmas Bargain
The Christmas Token
The Christmas Calamity
The Christmas Vow
The Christmas Quandary
The Christmas Confection
The Christmas Melody
The Christmas Ring
The Christmas Wish
The Christmas Kiss

Holiday Express
Holiday Hope
Holiday Heart
Holiday Home
Holiday Love

Boise, Idaho
May 1972

Ribbons of sunshine gliding through the leaves of the trees around her caressed Grace Marshall's cheek. Eyes closed, she tipped her head back to accept the gift of warmth and breathed deeply of the fresh air.

Thankfully, no one else was currently in the place used by the Boise Veterans Administration Hospital nurses as a break area when the weather was pleasant. Without the scent of cigarette smoke filling the air and the peaceful quiet of a spring day surrounding her, it was easy for Grace to block from her mind the challenging morning she'd endured, assisting an egotistical doctor with two impossible patients.

Grace turned on the transistor radio on the table, where she sat and listened as Otis Redding sang about sitting on the dock of a bay. She could sure use a vacation. What would it be like to head south, somewhere that already felt like summer, and dangle her feet in the water? Maybe spend an entire afternoon doing nothing but bathing in the sun and indulging in fruity drinks.

Then again, she could always head home to Holiday and sit with her feet in the water of one of the lovely lakes in the area. Her mom had a great strawberry lemonade recipe, and there was the pineapple punch she'd made for a birthday party last August that everyone still talked about.

Just thinking about her family in the Eastern Oregon community where she'd grown up made her lonesome to see her parents and brothers. Only Micah remained at home, though, helping with their dairy farm. Jared was with the Marines in Vietnam, although Grace had no idea of his current location. Jason was off at college in Corvallis, finishing his third year of working toward a degree in agribusiness.

As Grace bit into the roast beef sandwich loaded with pickles and celery her roommate had made for her that morning, she thought about how much she missed her mom's cheeseburger pie and chicken casserole. Grace had the recipes and could make them, but they never tasted quite the same.

She shook her head, attempting to dislodge her homesickness. She'd lived in Boise for three years, but there were still moments she longed to be back in Holiday, where the air smelled like Christmas and most everyone seemed like family.

In Boise, Grace often felt lost in the crowd, but she was finding her way and, she hoped, making life a little better for the patients she helped at the VA Hospital.

She glanced at the assortment of magazines on the table. Elizabeth Taylor and her grandson graced the cover of *Ladies' Home Journal*, along with promises for sew-and-go fashions that could be made in a day, if one had time for sewing. She glanced at an article about an opportunity to win a free vacation.

"Not likely," she muttered, took another bite of the sandwich, then picked up the latest copy of *McCall's* magazine. It offered nostalgic needlework ideas and had one of her favorite features—a bonus historical romance story. Grace loved to read; she just didn't get much time to enjoy it.

Quickly opening the magazine to the story, she was soon engrossed in the tale. It wasn't until she heard a chair squeak that she realized she was no longer alone.

"Hey, Susie. How are things going for you today?" she asked as she dabbed her mouth with a paper napkin, then took a drink of the Coca-Cola she'd purchased from the vending machine inside. Little droplets of condensation slid along the neck of the glass bottle as she tilted it to her lips.

"As good as can be," Susie said, reaching for the *Cosmopolitan* magazine and flipping it open before she folded back the waxed paper on her cheese sandwich and took a bite.

Grace returned to the story and her lunch, enjoying both before she glanced at the watch on her wrist and knew it was time to head back inside. How she wished she could yank off the white stockings she wore and bask in the sunshine this afternoon. Instead, she had plenty of patients to see and important work to do.

"See you later," she said to Susie, then gathered her things and returned inside.

An hour into her afternoon shift, she wished she'd stayed outside. One cranky patient had yelled at her when she'd tried to check his pulse, and one downright nasty man had threatened her just as the doctor walked in. Thankfully, Dr. O'Brien had asked her to send in one of the older nurses to deal with the unpleasant patient.

By the time her work wrapped up for the day, Grace was exhausted and more than ready to head back to the apartment she shared with her best friend.

She and Cindy Milton had been friends since they were old enough to walk. They were in the same grade in school and even had crushes on the same boy in their junior year of high school. However, Caleb had returned Cindy's affection. The two of them had been engaged to marry before he'd gotten himself killed in Vietnam.

Thoughts of the war always made Grace's heart feel as heavy as one of the anvils Cindy's grandfather kept in the old livery building in Holiday. She hated that so many young men had died. Almost as tragic was the way the returning soldiers were treated by so many, as though they had single-handedly caused the war. Political views aside, Grace thought anyone who fought for America deserved respect and gratitude.

She knew how hard it was on soldiers to go off to war, and not just from the men she treated at the hospital. Her father as well as her Uncle Thad had fought in World War II. While her father had survived his time spent in the Pacific battling the Japanese, Uncle Thad had been killed by a German bullet in France, leaving behind a wife and two children who missed him still. Although her father rarely talked about the war, Grace knew he still occasionally had nightmares that would wake them all in the stillness of the night.

The dark thoughts circling like vultures in her mind weren't appropriate for such a lovely day. When her shift ended, Grace stepped out into the bright spring sunshine and shrugged them away.

"Do you and Cindy have plans this evening?" Susie asked, falling into step with Grace as they walked across the lot where the staff parked.

"No. At least none of which I'm aware," Grace said with a grin. Cindy, who was full of fun, often talked her into spur-of-the-moment adventures.

"Well, after a busy day like today, on our feet at the beck and call of the doctors, I think we deserve a quiet evening to rest." Susie sighed as she set her purse inside her car and unpinned the hat from her short hair. "However, I have no doubt my husband will expect dinner on the table as usual."

"I hope you have a nice evening. See you tomorrow." Grace waved at Susie, then continued walking to her car, a hand-me-down from her oldest brother. Micah had bought the sporty two-door Chevrolet Impala brand new out of a showroom six years ago, but last fall, he'd purchased a new pickup and asked Grace if she'd like to have the car, no strings attached. She'd practically screamed in his ear when he'd phoned to offer the car to her. She'd loved it the moment Micah had driven it home, and she loved it even more now that it was hers.

Although the weather hadn't offered too many days warm enough to roll down the windows and let the wind blow through her hair, Grace looked forward to it this summer.

Like Susie, she unpinned the hat from her head and loosened the top two buttons of her uniform as she waited for Cindy.

Cindy didn't like to drive or own a vehicle and preferred it that way. Typically, though, her friend beat her to the car. Rather than linger in concern over why Cindy was late, Grace reached behind the seat and retrieved a paper tablet, scrounged a pen out of her purse, then started writing a letter to send to Jared.

It had been a while since she'd written to him. If she hurried, she could bake a batch of brown sugar drops tonight, then get a care package ready to mail to him tomorrow. She'd collected a few things she thought he might enjoy, like a new book Jason had recommended, and packages of Jared's favorite gum and candy. Jared loved Fruit Stripe gum and was the only one in their family who preferred Butter Rum Life Savers to any other flavor. Just for fun, she planned to include some Pixy Stix and a few boxes of Lemonhead candy.

Attention centered on the letter she wrote, describing the weather, the wall she and Cindy had painted in their apartment's bathroom, and family news he might not have heard, she sucked in a gasp when her friend yanked open the car door and plopped onto the passenger seat.

"Man, I am beat. Let's go home." Cindy set her purse between her feet and looked over at Grace. "You look awful." Her nose wrinkled. "And what is on your uniform?"

Grace glanced down at the stains on her dress and shook her head. "You don't want to know."

"You're right. I don't."

Grace ripped from the tablet the pages she'd written on and tucked them into her purse, then started the car. "Any side trips on the way home?"

"Not tonight." Cindy rolled down her window and rested her elbow on the door, drawing in a deep breath as she visibly relaxed. "Gosh, it was a long day, wasn't it?"

"No argument from me." Grace wondered what had happened to make her sunshiny friend look more like a raincloud. Cindy worked in the administrative offices at the hospital, but most often, she ended her workday with the same chipper attitude with which it began.

Grace might have found it highly annoying if she hadn't loved her friend so much. Cindy had always been sweet and cheerful. Even after losing her fiancé, she'd managed to offer comfort to those around her while she had stoically worked her way through her grief.

Two years later, Cindy remained alone and unattached, and Grace worried she might never date again, but if time truly healed all wounds, then perhaps love awaited Cindy somewhere in the future.

Love had proven to be quite an elusive thing, at least where Grace was concerned. Then again, she'd never been deeply in love with anyone. Not the way Cindy had loved and been loved. Grace longed to have that kind of soul connection with another and often dreamed of the day she might have a husband and family of her own. She was so busy with work and everything else in her life she didn't have much time or energy left for dating, even if she'd met someone who sparked her interest. Which she hadn't. Not yet. But a girl couldn't give up hoping to find true love.

She tried to recall the last time she'd been on a date as she drove to their apartment building located halfway between the hospital grounds and the Boise River near the zoo. The building was only a few years old, and the apartments had a long waiting list, but Cindy's uncle knew someone who was friends with the building manager and had gotten them into an apartment when they'd decided to move to Boise. It wasn't overly spacious, but it was clean and safe, and the rent was affordable.

"What do you think of noodle goulash for dinner?" Grace asked as she pulled into her parking space at the apartment building. It was her turn to cook since they traded off every other night. A trip to the grocery store would need to happen soon, but she thought they had enough ingredients to make the simple dish that was filling.

"As long as you're cooking, I'm all for it," Cindy said with a grin as she rolled up the window and got out, locking the door behind her.

Both sets of their parents had lectured them about being careful, taking precautions, and not assuming a bigger city like Boise, in comparison to their small town of Holiday, was always a safe place for two young women.

So far, neither of the girls had run into any trouble. Then again, they rarely stayed out late and avoided the seedier parts of town.

"I'm so glad tomorrow is Friday," Cindy said as she held open the door to the lobby.

"You and me both. I'm so grateful to be on a day schedule now. Working nights was terrible, and so was working weekends. I feel very fortunate to work in the office with Dr. O'Brien. Even Dr. Bernstein and Dr. Robinson are tolerable on most days."

Cindy nodded in agreement as they walked over to the mailboxes on the wall and retrieved their mail.

Grace glanced down at a note from the building manager letting her know she had a package to pick up. She held up the yellow notecard so Cindy could see it. "Want to come with me to retrieve whatever this is?"

"Sure."

Together, they made their way to the building manager's door down the hall on the main floor.

Grace knocked and listened as she heard someone holler that they were coming.

"Hey girls," the older man said as he pulled the door open with a smile. "Got a box right here for you, Miss Marshall."

"Thank you, Mr. Crocker." Grace handed him the notecard, then accepted the box he held out to her.

"It's got some weight to it. Postmark is Holiday. Assumed it must be from your folks."

Grace nodded, wondering if the snoopy old man had removed the brown paper wrapped around the box and investigated it or had managed to hold back his curiosity enough to let her be the first to open her own mail. "Thanks, Mr. Crocker. Have a nice evening."

"You girls do the same." He was already closing the door before they could turn around and head to the stairs. They lived on the second floor of the three-story building. The basement held a nice laundry facility, which was great since Grace had to wash her uniforms frequently. Grateful she had one clean dress to see her through her last shift of the week, she knew she'd spend part of her Saturday scrubbing stains out of the white fabric, then pressing the uniforms so they looked crisp and fresh.

"Wonder what you got?" Cindy asked as they made their way up the stairs, turned down the hall, and used her key to unlock their door.

"Whew! It's warm in here," Grace said, stepping inside and heading straight for the windows in the living area. She set her box and purse on the floor by the couch, pushed the curtain aside, and opened the window, letting in the fresh air.

Cindy did the same with the window in the kitchen before they both went to their rooms to change. The apartment offered a small kitchen with a little dining area between it and the living room. Two bedrooms were on either side of a short hallway with a bathroom located at the end. There was one closet in the hallway where they stored linens and another by the door where they kept their coats. The space was efficient if not roomy.

Grace gave Cindy a few moments in the bathroom, then grabbed a change of clothes. She took a shower, washing away the grime and sickness of the day, then slathered lotion on her skin that held a faint tropical fragrance. She tugged on a pair of worn jeans and a soft T-shirt before rushing to the kitchen.

Cindy stood at the stove browning the ground beef they'd need for the goulash.

"I said I'd cook," Grace admonished as she took out a large pot from a bottom cabinet. She filled it with water and then set it on a burner to boil.

"I know, but I'm starving. The sooner we get this ready, the sooner we can eat." Cindy grinned at her. "I'm also dying to know what is in the box you received and assumed you'd open it after dinner."

"You assume correctly. I'll open it right after we eat. While the goulash bakes, I want to whip up a batch of cookies for Jared."

At the mention of her brother, Cindy blushed.

That was new.

Grace knew Jared had written to Cindy a few times after her fiancé was killed, but had her brother been writing to her best friend more frequently than she realized? If romance was brewing between Cindy and Jared, it would make Grace deliriously happy. She'd dreamed so many times of Cindy becoming her sister. In a small town with three handsome brothers, the odds had been in her favor, but Cindy had always loved Caleb.

Now, though, with just the very mention of Jared's name making her friend's cheeks turn pink, Grace could hardly hold her tongue, wanting to know if romance was afoot, but she wouldn't say anything. At least not yet.

"I thought if I baked the cookies tonight, I could box up a care package. I can mail it tomorrow on my lunch break."

"That's a great idea, Grace. I'm happy to help."

Grace bit her tongue to keep from teasing Cindy and merely nodded her head in thanks.

While Cindy finished cooking the ground beef with chopped onion, thinly sliced celery, and salt, Grace drained the noodles, then stirred them with tomato sauce and added it to the meat mixture. She spooned the meat and noodles into a casserole dish, added shredded cheese on top, then slid it into the oven. In about twenty minutes, they'd have a hot, filling meal with enough leftovers that they wouldn't have to cook tomorrow night.

Grace washed the dishes they'd dirtied while Cindy got out their baking sheets and set out ingredients to make cookies.

"Brown sugar drops?" Cindy asked as she retrieved brown sugar from the refrigerator and set it on the countertop.

"That's what I had planned." Grace set the skillet she'd just dried back on the stove, then hurried to cream together shortening and eggs while Cindy measured the sugar and flour. Working together, it didn't take long to have the cookies ready to slide into the oven.

While Cindy set the table, Grace made a green salad with the last of their lettuce, a stubby end of a cucumber, and a few radishes. How she longed to pluck a fresh radish from her mother's garden, brush away the rich earth, and bite into it.

For now, what they could buy at the grocery store would have to do.

Truly, Grace was thankful she and Cindy could share the apartment and expenses. She knew they fared better than many young women living on their own. It helped that Grace's brother had provided her with a car, and both of their families had donated a motley assortment of furniture for them to use.

Grace glanced at their couch, which had once belonged to her grandparents, and the table and dining chairs that had once sat in the Miltons' home. There wasn't a single piece of new furniture in the place, but somehow it all worked together.

She looked around the apartment, at least what she could see from her spot in the kitchen. The walls in the living room and bedrooms were painted a soft cream color instead of some ghastly modern hue. The kitchen cupboards were pale maple, the countertops white, and the wallpaper was a dainty pattern of flowers on a white background, giving the space an old-fashioned charm.

"Is it ready?" Cindy asked, filling two glasses with iced tea and carrying them to the table. "I'm so hungry, I might start gnawing on the silverware."

"You aren't the only one." Grace grinned over her shoulder as she pulled the casserole from the oven and carried it to the table. She slid the cookie sheets into the warm oven and retrieved the salad, then the two of them sat down and bowed their heads. Grace offered a brief word of thanks for their meal, then they dug into it, discussing their day and the problems they'd both experienced at work.

By the time they finished eating, the cookies were baked, and cooling on a rack. Grace washed the dishes, while Cindy dried them, then they returned to the living room.

"Will you open it now?" Cindy pointed to the box on the floor at the end of the couch.

Grace was as curious as her friend to find out what was inside the box, but she wanted to make the anticipation last as long as possible.

However, the box would be perfect to use to send Jared's care package, so if she wanted to pack it tonight to have it ready to mail to him, she needed to open it and discover what her family had sent to her.

"Fine," Grace feigned indifference as she opened the sewing box they kept beneath the coffee table and took out a pair of silver swan-neck scissors that had once belonged to her great-grandmother. She used the sharp tip to cut the string around the box, and pulled away the brown paper, which was a grocery sack. Her economical mother had trimmed off the bottom and slit up the side of a bag to wrap the box. Grace could turn it over and use it to wrap Jared's package.

She opened the box to find a note on top of what appeared to be a finely crafted mahogany case.

"What is it?" Cindy asked, leaning over the throw pillow on the couch to see into the box.

"I'm not sure," Grace said, quickly opening the note that was written in her father's bold hand.

Dear Gracie,
When I was in Salem at the dairymen's meeting last week, I wandered into a store selling vintage items, which I never do. We have enough of our own junk at home without paying good money for someone else's cast-offs.

Grace smiled, envisioning her father wandering through a shop filled with turn-of-the-century treasures and snarling at each thing he encountered.

Don't ask me what or why I felt compelled to go into that store, but the moment I saw this, I knew you had to have it. Not only is it pretty, but it will also come in handy if you ever need to defend yourself. Also, the clerk who sold it to me said it once belonged to Adelaide Brennan—the actress I've always been so fond of watching. I have no idea how the gun wound up in Salem, but it seems to have quite a storied past. Ironically enough, it has even been in Holiday before, in the possession of one of our relatives. There's a note in the pocket inside the case you should read. Use this key to open it.

We miss you, baby girl, and hope life is good there. Looking forward to your next visit.

Love you,
Dad

P.S. Your mother mailed a letter to you yesterday, so if you haven't received it yet, it should arrive shortly. You can get all the gossip from her.

"Wow!" Grace said, setting aside her father's note, lifting the case from the box, and setting it on her lap.

"Is that a gun case?" Cindy asked, leaning closer as the two of them examined the ornate pink mother-of-pearl inlay in the lid.

Grace reverently smoothed her fingers across it before she lifted the little brass key on a tarnished silver chain from the envelope that had held her father's note and inserted it into the lock on the case.

The click echoed throughout the room as she and Cindy held their breaths, anxious to see what treasure the case contained.

"Oh, my," Cindy said when Grace lifted the lid to reveal a pistol made with pink mother-of-pearl grips that appeared to match the lid of the case. "Why on earth did your family send this to you?"

"Dad sent it. Apparently, he found it in a junk store in Salem when he was recently at a dairymen's meeting. According to what he wrote in the letter, he bought it because I need protection, the gun is pretty, and it was supposedly owned by an actress he likes."

Cindy grinned. "Was it Adelaide Brennan? Your dad seems quite smitten with her. He practically runs over people in his haste to get to the television if one of her movies comes on."

Grace laughed, knowing what Cindy said wasn't much of an exaggeration. "It was Miss Adelaide. The woman has to be what, close to eighty now?"

"I would think so," Cindy agreed, then motioned to the pistol. "I've never seen anything so pretty and deadly. It's like a Wild West weapon tangled with something entirely feminine."

"Dad said there's a note in the pocket that explains about the gun." Grace found the pocket in the lining of the case and gently extracted a letter that was growing yellow with age.

The words were written with a type of penmanship she'd only seen on postcards and notes sent by her relatives from decades ago.

She who possesses this pistol possesses an opportunity that must not be squandered. Cast in the tender dreams of maidens from ages past, the steel of this weapon is steadfast and true and will lead an unmarried woman to a man forged from the same virtuous elements. One need only fit her hand to the grip and open her heart to activate the promise for which this pistol was fashioned—the promise of true love. Patience and courage will illuminate her path. Hope and faith will guide her steps until her heart finds its home.

Once the promise is fulfilled, the bearer must release the pistol and pass it to another or risk losing what she has found.
Accept the gift . . . or not.
Believe its promise . . . or not.
But hoard the pistol for personal gain . . . and lose what you hold most dear.

"Well, that's quite a ... warning." Cindy grinned again. "What do you think? If you hold the pistol and make a wish, will Prince Charming come knocking at our door?"

Grace scowled at her. "Not likely. For goodness' sake, who believes in such silliness?" She glanced down and noticed more writing on the aged parchment.

A gift from the great Annie Oakley, this pistol carries a legacy of love. If you possess this pistol and find love, please record your name and a bit of your story to encourage those who follow.
Tessa James married Jackson Spivey on March 3, 1894, in Caldwell, Texas - I was aiming for his heart but accidentally winged him in the arm. Thankfully, forgiveness and love cover a multitude of mishaps.
Rena Burke wed Josh Gatlin on June 2, 1894, in Holiday, Oregon – When my trousers and target practice didn't send him running, I knew true love had hit the perfect target for me.

"Oh, my stars!" Grace gasped, pointing to the paper. "Look, Cindy! It's Rena Burke. She was a cousin to my great-grandpa, Theo Marshall."

"What?" Cindy read the note and shook her head. "How could this be? How could this pistol go from what appears to be Texas to Holiday to all these other places, then end up in a store in Salem where your dad just happened to find it? What are the odds of that happening?"

"Maybe it's not odds. Maybe a little divine intervention nudged Dad to go to that store and buy this." Grace knew it sounded far-fetched, perhaps even whimsical and fantastical, but the thought that one of her long-ago relatives had held this pistol in her hand, not to mention the legendary Annie Oakley, made her take the note more seriously.

She read it again. The last entry was from 1955.

Rexanna Brennan married Roan Bertoletti on September 29, 1955. I've shot exotic game worthy of the finest of trophies, but my cowboy's love has been my biggest prize of all.

Brennan. She wondered if Rexanna Brennan was related to the actress her father adored. If so, it made sense how the woman would have been in possession of the gun.

But what about all the other women who'd owned it in the past? Could the words penned all those years ago hold truth? According to the instructions, all Grace needed to do was hold it in her hand and open her heart to love.

That sounded easy enough. She certainly wasn't opposed to love, even if she hadn't found it yet.

While it might seem trivial to believe in such nonsense, a little voice in the back of her mind reminded her she didn't have anything to lose by trying.

She certainly couldn't get more alone than she already was unless Cindy suddenly decided to leave her, which she knew wasn't about to happen. Not when the two of them were closer than sisters.

Grace folded the letter and returned it to the pocket in the case's lining, lifted the pistol in her hand, and closed her eyes. She remained silent, letting the thoughts roll through her mind. *"I open my heart to the possibility of love, to the hope that somewhere out there is a man who'll love me truly, fiercely, faithfully, and tenderly for the rest of my life, and when he comes along, I'll be wise enough to realize it's him."*

Cindy hopped off the couch and made a great show of racing across the room and pressing her ear to the door while Grace returned the pistol to the case, tucking the key inside before she closed the lid.

"What are you doing?" Grace asked as Cindy pretended to be listening for footsteps.

"Eagerly awaiting the approach of true love." Cindy giggled. "Do you think Mr. Crocker will let your prince ride his white charger up the stairs?"

Grace rolled her eyes and lobbed a pillow at Cindy. "Come away from the door, you loon, and help me pack this box for Jared."

As the two of them worked to fill a tin with the cookies and pack treats and essentials Jared would appreciate into the box, Grace's thoughts swirled around the pink pistol and the legend of love it had so unexpectedly brought into her life.

Later, when she settled into bed, she closed her eyes and drifted to sleep, contemplating what it might be like to finally fall in love.

"No, Ma, I don't need you to go with me."

"But honey, are you sure you should be driving the pickup … like that?"

Levi Gibson tried not to glower as his mother's gaze drifted from his eyes to his hand, or what was left of it.

As a soldier in Vietnam, one minute he'd been walking through waist-high grass with the rest of the men in his unit; the next, he'd heard a loud whistle followed by a blast that blew him off his feet. He hadn't paid any mind to his injuries as he'd grabbed a soldier whose leg had been blown off, tossed the man over his shoulder, and run for cover.

He'd left the soldier with other wounded men out of harm's way, prepared to run back and see if anyone else needed help, when someone tackled him from behind and rolled him on the ground. It wasn't until the flames had been extinguished that Levi understood his sleeve was on fire, searing the cloth into his skin.

The next thing he remembered was waking up in a medical tent with his left hand and arm bandaged. The worst part of it all was that he'd always been left-handed. Now, with just his thumb and forefinger and a small part of his palm remaining, he was forced to learn to do everything right-handed, and he hated it.

His handwriting looked like he'd failed first-grade penmanship. Grabbing onto things or opening jars proved to be a challenge. He found it nearly impossible to button anything. Thankfully, he mostly wore T-shirts at home and western shirts with snaps when he went into town.

As a fourth-generation farmer, he'd never wanted to leave the rich ground his family farmed in Star, Idaho, a short drive from the state capital of Boise. After raising potatoes for decades, about ten years ago, they'd diversified by putting a third of their ground into sugar beets. That was when his uncle had decided to branch out on his own and moved his family to Pasco, Washington, where he'd started his own potato farm.

Levi had missed his cousins, but he'd worked hard to earn his father's respect. He'd been just twenty-one when his father had changed the name of their business to Gibson & Son Farms. It had been one of the proudest days of Levi's life.

Then he'd felt the call of duty and enlisted to help fight in Vietnam. His first tour of duty had been tolerable, but the second had been nothing but one disaster after another. One of his fellow soldiers had carried a Zippo lighter inscribed, "We the unwilling, led by the unqualified to kill the unfortunate, die for the ungrateful."

He'd come to think every word of it was true. Honestly, Levi was surprised he'd made it home alive, even if he carried scars, both the visible and those unseen, that had lacerated his soul.

War was not for the faint-hearted, that much was certain. The things he'd seen and experienced over there would haunt him for the rest of his life. Of that, he had no doubt.

He'd found it difficult to return home, wounded and broken, and try to fit back into the mold his parents had created for him as their only child and heir to a large farm that turned a good profit most years.

"Maybe I should drive you," Levi's mother offered, rising from the oak dining chair where she'd been seated, drinking a cup of coffee in her sunny kitchen. The house, originally built back in 1910, looked Victorian on the outside and used to look that way on the inside as well. About six years ago, his mother had taken an interior decorating class with a friend. The two of them had turned the inside of the house into something that came straight from one of the ladies' magazines his mother so enjoyed reading.

She'd gone for a western theme in the living room with leather couches and chairs that had what appeared to be wagon wheels on the ends of them. The end tables and even the chandelier had a wagon-wheel theme.

The white kitchen cabinets had been removed, and new wooden cabinets had taken their place. Levi and his father had both been more than a little surprised to discover his mother had selected all pink appliances. Every time she opened the door to the pink oven, Levi wanted to laugh. It looked like a doll house kitchen, but his mother was a good cook, so he couldn't complain about the results, even if the color scheme wasn't one that he particularly appreciated.

"I'll be fine, Ma, but thanks for offering." Levi tried to keep the irritation and exasperation out of his voice. Since he'd returned home almost six months ago, his mother had babied and coddled him until he thought he might implode.

After three weeks of her well-meaning but incredibly annoying care, he'd decided to move into the house vacated by his uncle's family on the other side of the farm. The house gave him some much-needed privacy and quiet but kept him close enough to check in with his parents every day. He typically ate dinner at their house and often breakfast, which seemed to please his mother immensely.

Since his uncle's house, a Craftsman home that had been built in the 1920s, had sat empty so long, it had needed a lot of work and updating, but it had been a project that had helped Levi in body, mind, and spirit. He'd found something therapeutic in pounding nails and ripping off old shingles. During the winter months, his father had helped him with much of the needed work, but he deferred to Levi about every decision that was made in regard to the house slowly turning into a home.

One thing Levi knew for certain: he had no interest at all in letting his mother help him decorate the interior. She'd handed him a box full of wallpaper and paint samples as well as interior decorating magazines a few weeks ago. He'd taken a glance at the funky colors and tossed the whole thing in the garbage. He needed calm, peaceful surroundings, not poppy red walls with school bus yellow furniture and lights that looked like they came from outer space.

He had plans to restore the house to how it initially looked when his grandparents had built it fifty years ago, and nothing in the home had been bright red or yellow, or even that sickly shade of avocado green that seemed to be growing in popularity. He certainly wasn't going to allow his mother to turn the kitchen into her idea of a pink or turquoise baker's paradise.

Everything was already planned out in his mind, if not on paper. The bedrooms upstairs had all been painted, as had the rooms downstairs. For the most part, he'd chosen white paint. The large living room, dining room, and foyer he'd painted a light, almost buttery yellow hue, accenting it with white trim. His dad had told him it looked like something from an architectural digest, which pleased Levi immensely. He'd given the big bedroom on the main floor a soft, calming shade of blue that made him think of a springtime sky. The kitchen walls had the barest hint of green, contrasting nicely with the white cupboards he'd recently installed.

Levi had hired an electrician to rewire everything and install a new furnace. His father's friend, a plumber by trade, had come a month ago and updated all the plumbing, even adding an outdoor sink on the back porch, where Levi could wash up before he trailed mud or dirt into the house.

Maybe someday he'd have a wife who appreciated that, but he doubted it. A woman would have to be completely desperate or entirely crazy to want to get mixed up with him. Levi felt like he'd returned home less than a whole man, one with nasty burn scars up his arm, a deformed stump for a hand, and nightmares that often plagued him even during the daylight hours. A sound or noise, or even a smell, could unexpectedly yank him back to his time in Vietnam, leaving him disoriented. Sometimes he'd awaken after completely blacking out. So far, he'd done his best to hide his troubles from his parents.

Occasionally, he found himself irritable and short-tempered, particularly with his mother, for no apparent reason. Then again, his father hinted that Stella Gibson could try the patience of a saint from time to time.

Levi smirked as he recalled his father's sage words of wisdom, then turned away from his mom lest she see his humor and prod to unearth the reason for his smile.

"I promise I can drive to the appointment and back with no trouble, Ma. I've done it any number of times." Levi started to pour a cup of coffee, then decided he was jittery enough without adding caffeine to his system.

"But this is the first time you'll be driving your new pickup in Boise, honey. You have to shift it." She grabbed an imaginary gear shift and shoved her hand forward while stomping both feet to the floor. If that's how she handled a vehicle with a clutch, it was no wonder his father never asked her to help drive any of the farm equipment.

Levi rubbed his good hand over the back of his neck, doing his best to hold back the testy words that danced on his tongue. "I'll be fine, Ma. Now, is there anything I can bring you from town?"

"Are you sure you don't mind, honey?" Stella rose from the table and retrieved a pad she kept by the wall telephone located near the kitchen door. She tore off the top page, added a few things in an ornately flourished script, then held the paper out to him.

"I'm happy to run by the store for you, Ma. It's on my way home, anyway." Levi took the piece of paper and stuffed it into his shirt pocket, then moved a step back. "I better get going."

"I'd be happy to drive you, Levi. It would just …"

"Stell! Leave the boy be," Gary Gibson said as he stepped into the kitchen through the back door and tugged off the dusty John Deere ball cap he wore on his head.

Levi nodded once to his dad and then hurried out the door before his mother changed her mind and went with him.

He was nearly to the new orange and white Chevy pickup he'd parked at the end of the walk when he heard the screen door squawk behind him. He looked back to see his father grinning at him. "Can you run by the equipment shop on your way home, son? I phoned in an order for parts for the 4020 tractor. It should be ready to pick up on your way home."

"Sure thing, Pop. See you after a while."

His father lifted a hand. "Take your time. No need to rush. Maybe you'll meet a pretty girl or two and want to take them for a soda or out for lunch."

"Right on, Pop." He might have sounded enthused, but Levi thought the odds of him meeting a girl who would give him the time of day were somewhere between zero and none.

He started the pickup and headed down the long driveway toward the road that would take him into Star. One of the reasons Levi had chosen this particular model of pickup was due to the slim steering wheel. It was easy for him to wrap his left finger and thumb around it, leaving his right hand free for shifting or fiddling with the radio to pick up the signal, which was what he did as soon as he hit the main road.

When his favorite country station came in relatively clear, he relaxed against the leather bench seat embossed with acanthus scrolls and listened to Johnny Cash sing about a boy named Sue. The song was funny and clever and made him grin as he slowed when he hit the outskirts of Star and drove through town.

From classes in school, he knew Star had been one of the earliest settlements in the Boise area. A settler named Ben F. Swalley had arrived in 1863 with a team of oxen pulling his wagon and claimed three hundred acres of land along the Boise River, about a mile from where the town was now located. Other settlers joined him, and farms began to sprout up all around the area. One of the later branches of the Oregon Trail that crossed the river near Boise passed through the town. Portions of that early Oregon Trail corridor became a road connecting Boise to the town of Caldwell. A stage route eventually followed the road all the way to Umatilla, Oregon, and the Columbia River.

The town of Star got its name, though, from the first schoolhouse built on land donated from Swalley in the 1870s. One of the settlers sawed out a star and nailed it to the schoolhouse door. The star became a landmark for travelers, and the community became known as Star. The town was incorporated in 1905 and established the city limits four miles in all directions.

Levi's fourth-grade teacher, Miss Emma, would be proud he'd remembered all the local history she'd drilled into his head.

He drove through town, watching people come and go from the shops—some old, some new, descriptions which applied to both the shops and the people.

He considered stopping by Jackson's on his way home just to see what he might find. The store carried a little bit of everything and reminded him of what a mercantile might have looked like back in the early years of the century. A shopper could find everything from tin cups and mining equipment to kerosene lamps, old pickle crocks, tin advertisement signs, and barrels full of penny candy that now cost a nickel.

Levi drove through town, waving at people he recognized. At least here, in his small hometown, no one spit on him or called him a devil or any of the other horrible things that had happened to him when he'd first returned to the States and ventured from the hospital where he'd been recuperating. Some of the names he'd been called had been so vile that his ears still burned just thinking about them.

It had boggled his mind to see people who proclaimed themselves to be peace-loving turn so violent at the sight of someone from the military. It seemed the moment they caught sight of his uniform, they felt it their duty and right to list all the many ways he was a terrible person instead of making him feel like his sacrifice and service had meant something, that the lives of his friends who had died hadn't been in vain.

Levi sighed as he shifted into high gear and headed toward Boise. He listened as John Denver sang about country roads taking him home. That song had been an anthem of sorts to Levi during the days of his recuperation. All he'd wanted was to drive the country road that led to the home where he'd grown up.

Now that he was back in Star and on the farm, he sometimes questioned if he should have stayed away. His parents, mainly his mother, acted as though he was broken beyond repair. He didn't know if it was true or not, but at times, it sure felt that way.

Although he was only twenty-six, there were days he felt twice his age. It wasn't just the aches and pains in his body but the seeping wounds in his soul that made him feel mature beyond his years.

No one could go to war and return with their innocence and naivety still intact. No one.

Determined not to let the darkness of his experiences in Vietnam dim the pleasure of driving his new pickup on such a beautiful spring day, Levi rolled down his window, breathed in the scents of fresh rural air, and released a long breath.

It was definitely far too nice to spend the day dwelling in the past. Nothing he could do now would change a thing. It wouldn't restore his hand or his mind. It wouldn't bring his friends back from the dead, so there was little point in dwelling on the "if only's."

Levi drove past the Idaho State Capitol in Boise before he turned and headed to the VA Hospital. The doctor wanted him to come in every six weeks for a checkup just to make sure his wounds were healing properly and, Levi thought, to gauge his mental state.

As he headed toward old Fort Boise, where the hospital was located, he recalled his history lessons about the fort being abandoned before the First World War and loaned to the U.S. Public Health Service to care for the soldiers returning from the war. After Congress passed a hospital bill in 1922 providing health care for veterans, the Public Health

Service Hospital turned over operations to the Veterans Bureau on an indefinite lease, and the Veterans Hospital was founded.

"Boy, Miss Emma would give me a gold star today," Levi said with a sardonic grin as he pulled into the parking lot and found an empty spot on the far side of the lot. He had two good legs on which he could walk and wouldn't dream of taking a space someone else might need closer to the door.

Levi dreaded these appointments. Not because he wasn't healing, but because of the pitying glances and sympathetic looks the medical staff offered. He didn't want or need anyone's pity. In some ways, it bothered him more than the anger of the protestors ever had.

Inside the hospital, he removed his cowboy hat and held it in his damaged hand, hoping the missing parts of it wouldn't be as noticeable beneath the brim as he checked in at the front desk, then made his way upstairs to see his doctor.

In the waiting room, he gave his name and pertinent information to the woman at the receptionist's desk, then took a seat with a handful of other men who looked equally as displeased to be there. A man in the corner of the room looked rough, like he'd been sleeping on the street. His clothes and skin were filthy, and his stench filled the space with a stale, ripe odor.

Thankful there were empty seats on the other side of the room, Levi sank onto one of the chairs and impatiently waited, bouncing one leg until the older man sitting next to him tapped his knee with a rolled-up magazine.

"If you don't mind, I'd like what innards I have left to not be shaken to death before I can get out of here."

"Sorry, sir," Levi said, chagrined. He sat up straighter in the chair and tipped his head politely to the man. "What branch did you serve in, sir?"

"Marines. World War II. Ever heard of the Bataan Death March?"

"I have, sir. It was a horrible thing."

"It was like living in a nightmare, but I'm glad I survived. I think my wife was too." The man grinned at him.

Levi held out his hand to the former soldier, grateful when he shook it. "Thank you for your service, sir."

The older man nodded. "What about you? Just back from 'Nam?"

"Army. Returned stateside about nine months ago. Spent some time healing up before they let me come home." Levi gave the older man a studying glance, wondering if he was nearly as old as he appeared or if the terror he'd endured during the war had aged him prematurely. "I have to come in periodically so they can poke and prod me."

The older man chuckled. "Same here. Lieutenant James Jepson, but my friends call me J.J."

"Nice to meet you, sir. Sergeant Levi Gibson, but my friends don't call me anything because most of them are dead." Levi had no idea why he'd spoken so bluntly and wished he could reel the words back in.

J.J. lifted a gnarled hand and patted Levi on the shoulder, not in sympathy, but in commiseration. "I'm sorry, son."

"Thanks, sir."

"James Jepson!" a nurse called, standing in the doorway that led back to the examination rooms. "James Jepson!"

The old man lifted his hand and pushed himself upward. He patted one shirt pocket, then the other, and extracted a card with his name and phone number neatly printed on it. "You ever want to talk, son, soldier to soldier or man to man, just give me a call."

"Thank you, sir." Levi rose and shook his hand again before resuming his seat. He watched J.J. walk toward the nurse with a noticeable limp, then returned to impatiently awaiting his turn.

He could see two nurses engaged in a heated discussion carried out in whispers. They both kept looking at the guy in the corner who smelled like rank garbage. It wasn't hard to imagine they were arguing over which one of them had to deal with him.

Finally, the older of the two marched out of the office and soon returned with two orderlies who had on rubber gloves and big aprons covering their clothes.

"Corporal Daniels, before the doctor can see you, you'll need to clean up. These men will show you where you can take a shower."

The man, who had to be homeless, started to shake his head.

Levi was convinced he saw bugs fall out of Corporal Daniels' hair onto the floor beneath his chair.

"We insist," one of the orderlies said, clasping the man's thin arm and gently pulling him to his feet. The moment they had him out the door, the elderly nurse wiped down the chair where he'd been sitting with what Levi had to assume was disinfectant, then did the same for the floor.

Relieved to see the corporal would get the help he obviously needed, Levi mused over how much worse his situation could be. He had family who cared about him. His mind was mostly functioning, even if nightmares invaded it more than they should. He had plenty of good food to eat, a nice place to live, and money to buy what he needed. Guilt assailed him for not appreciating what he had instead of focusing so much on what had been taken from him.

Lost in his thoughts, he almost missed hearing a nurse call his name. He stood and turned to stare at one of the prettiest girls he'd seen in a long, long while—maybe ever.

Rich brown hair was pulled back in a no-nonsense bun at the back of her head, with her nurse's cap perched just so. Her white uniform, stockings, and sensible shoes looked crisp and fresh, and her tone sounded melodic as she called his name a second time.

His gaze collided with her warm hazel eyes, then drifted down to observe her flawless, milky skin, berry-hued lips, rosy cheeks, and stubborn chin above a long, delicate neck.

She was definitely the prettiest girl he'd ever seen. No question about it.

"I'm Levi," he said in a voice suddenly grown raspy, then cleared his throat as she motioned for him to follow her.

Levi didn't want her attending to him. Didn't want this sweet, lovely girl to see his burns or worse—his deformed hand. What would she think of him once she saw all that?

Where was the crotchety old nurse who'd been there the last few times he'd come in for appointments? He could handle her because he didn't care a whit what she thought of him.

But this girl? This young woman who was tall and graceful and lovely?

He didn't want to see the pity in her eyes or a look of disgust she would surely be unable to hide when she examined his hand.

"How does this day find you, Sergeant Gibson?" she asked in that melodic voice that he found both soothing and invigorating.

"Well enough," Levi said, moving into an examination room and taking a seat on the exam table as she indicated. "Call me, Levi, please? I feel like I left Sergeant Gibson behind ... over there."

She nodded as though she understood what over there meant and wouldn't ask questions. As she opened his chart and read through notes, he noticed her nametag.

RN G. Marshall.

He wondered what the G stood for. Glorious? Gorgeous? He knew RN meant she'd gone to school and was a Registered Nurse.

"All right, Levi. May I help you remove your shirt? The doctor will want to examine your arm, and I need to take your blood pressure."

Levi knew the routine. He used his right hand to yank open the snaps on his chambray shirt and slip it off his arm without exposing his hand since it still held his cowboy hat.

Before he could protest, though, the nurse snagged his hat from him, hung it on the hooks by the door, divested him of his shirt and hung it next to his hat, then wrapped a blood pressure cuff around his right arm as though she hadn't noticed his misshapen hand or his scars.

Levi felt angry, embarrassed, humiliated, and emasculated all at the same time. It wasn't a good combination. Volatile might be a better word to describe it.

He grumbled under his breath as she stuck the stethoscope in her ears and pumped the cuff until it felt like a tourniquet around his arm, which made him mumble all the more about the medical staff being too young, incompetent, and impertinent to know what they were doing.

She hiked one well-shaped, expressive eyebrow upward as she made notes in his chart, but that was the only indication she'd paid any mind to his mutterings. Covertly, he watched as she walked over to a drawer, extracted a thermometer, and shook it.

He held his lips tightly pressed together, unwilling to let her place it in his mouth.

Her gaze narrowed, and she held the thermometer in front of his face. "I can either stick this in your mouth, or you can drop those jeans, and we'll do it the hard way. It's up to you, buckaroo."

Surprise made him blink three times in succession, but he hastily opened his mouth. He caught a whiff of something that smelled tropical, like flowers combined with pineapples and coconut, as she stuck the thermometer in his mouth, then turned back to the drawer, extracting a tongue depressor and a few other things he detested but endured at these appointments.

"All right, let's see," she said, turning back around and looking at the thermometer. "Hmm. It appears to be normal, despite your flushed face." The look she gave him left no doubt in his mind that she'd thought him a bad-mannered hothead.

Not that she was entirely wrong. He should have kept his mouth shut, even if he thought she wouldn't hear what he uttered.

However, he refused to apologize. Not when she left him feeling flustered and mortified to be there. If he'd met this girl years ago before he'd enlisted, his heart had been broken, and life had been forever altered, he wouldn't have hesitated to ask her out for a date.

Now, though, he couldn't envision her giving him the time of day if she weren't forced to interact with him as his nurse.

Still, it rankled and rubbed him in all the wrong directions to have such a pretty nurse, one who looked so full of vitality and energy, seeing him when he felt so vulnerable and exposed. Everything in him wanted to yank on his shirt and leave.

"Levi!" Dr. Charles O'Brien said as he bustled into the room with a broad smile. "How are you feeling, son?"

"Fine, sir," Levi said, returning the doctor's smile. The first doctor he'd seen at the Boise VA Hospital had been a distracted oaf who'd barely even acknowledged him and certainly didn't listen to his concerns. The next time he'd gone in, he'd been given an appointment with Dr. O'Brien and liked him immediately. After meeting him, Levi had requested the jovial man become his primary physician, and so far, he had been.

"Let's have a look at you." The doctor peered into his mouth and down his throat, looked into his ears and eyes, felt along his neck, listened to his heart and lungs, then picked up Levi's left arm and ran gentle fingers over the thick scar tissue. The wounds had all closed, but the scars still ached from time to time. To him, they looked grotesque, like mangled, melted wax instead of flesh.

Dr. O'Brien worked his way down to Levi's hand, spending far more time on it than Levi liked as he spoke to the nurse, relaying medical terms, which she jotted down in his chart.

"You're coming right along, Levi. Everything looks good. Let's see about your range of motion."

The doctor had him move his arm in a series of exercises that Levi executed twice a day at home. A few pulled against his healing skin with a tautness that made him want to grimace in pain, but he kept his expression neutral and finished the last movement. The doctor then instructed him to move his left thumb and remaining finger, turning them this way and that.

"Excellent, son. That's excellent. How is the house remodel coming?" the doctor asked as he pushed his glasses back up on his nose.

Levi was both surprised and impressed the man had remembered they'd talked about his work on the house the last time he'd been in for an appointment.

"Coming along, sir. I have new electrical wiring and plumbing, the kitchen cabinets are installed, and the painting is complete. I'm just hoping to finish up before my mother decides I need her help."

Dr. O'Brien chuckled and thumped him on the back. "Considering the fact that I've met your mother, I'll wish you luck."

"Thanks, sir."

The doctor made a few notes in the chart, handed it back to the nurse, then smiled at Levi. "We'll see you again in six weeks."

"Yes, sir."

The doctor left the room, but Levi wanted to argue about the need to return so soon. To insist the appointments were unnecessary. Regardless, it made him feel marginally better to hear the doctor say he was healing well.

The only problem, though, was the fact that he hadn't counted on meeting a spunky young nurse with soulful eyes. When she smiled, her face transformed from pretty into beautiful, showing off exquisite cheekbones. If life were different—he were different—he sure wouldn't have hesitated to ask her out.

Now, though, he just wanted to escape her presence.

As though she sensed his thoughts, she reached behind her and lifted his shirt. She held it out for him to slip his arms into the sleeves.

The very idea of having her help him dress incensed Levi. That simple act smacked of him being an invalid. A victim. Weak. Needy.

And he wouldn't stand for it.

With a fierce glower, he snatched the shirt from her hands and rammed his arms into the sleeves. The hint of her tropical fragrance teased his senses, further infuriating him as he reached behind her for his hat. He stormed out of the office, shirt tails flapping in the breeze created by his fuming stride.

Angry with himself, angry at the world, he got into his pickup and sped back toward Star. He was nearly home before he remembered he needed to go pick up parts for his dad and groceries for his mother.

Checking to make sure no one was coming, he turned around in the road and roared back into town. As he drove, a vision of a lovely brown-haired nurse refused to budge from his head. How dare that woman make him feel like a bumbling fool!

3

"You need to tell me the story again. Start at the beginning."

Grace sighed as she started her car and backed out of the parking space at the hospital. After the cowboy had come in that morning, muttering about her being young, incompetent, and impertinent, then practically ripped his shirt from her hands and left in a huff, the day had gone from bad to worse.

One patient had lost his cool and nearly socked her in the jaw with a wild right hook when she'd had to give him a shot. Thank goodness growing up with three ornery brothers had given her fast reflexes. She'd dealt with a violently vomiting patient after that and one with a sore oozing putrid pus. And then there was the patient who …

Grace refused to think about what that last one had done in the exam room. At least she didn't have to clean up the messes, but she felt pity for the staff who did. Anxious to get home, shower, change, and block the day from her mind, she should never have mentioned to Cindy about seeing the cowboy that morning.

Sergeant Levi Gibson, a burn victim who was missing part of his hand, was an incredibly healthy and virile male specimen despite his injuries. From what Grace had observed, he hated to feel weak or vulnerable. She should have known better than to try to help with his shirt. Her brothers would have reacted no differently if it had been one of them.

Despite his thick blond hair that waved in the front, gorgeous blue eyes, handsome face, and muscular physique, she'd been downright affronted and agitated with him for what he'd said under his breath. Surely, he had to know she could hear the insults.

Grace had graduated at the top of her nursing class. She'd worked hard at her job and gave so much of herself to her patients. To have someone accuse her of being too young to do her job, someone she knew for a fact was only a year older than she, had made her bite her tongue to keep from setting the former soldier on his ear.

Something about him had gotten to her, though. There was nothing unusual about seeing a half-clad patient, but the moment Levi Gibson had removed his shirt, her mouth had gone dry, and she'd fought an internal battle to reach out and touch his tanned, muscled bicep.

Instead of surrendering to it, she'd slapped a blood pressure cuff around his arm and gotten so distracted by studying his thick eyelashes that she'd pumped the cuff longer than she should have, but she sure wasn't going to admit that to him. Not when he'd come off as peevish and prideful.

Heaven help any woman dealing with a man's wounded ego or pride.

Despite her first impression of Sergeant Gibson, Dr. O'Brien had clearly thought well of him. Charles O'Brien was one of the few doctors who worked at the VA Hospital who didn't treat Grace like she had feathers for brains. She found him to be jolly, kind, skilled, and patient.

When she'd asked him in passing about Levi, the doctor had grinned at her and said, "He's a nice-looking young man, isn't he? If I had any single daughters left to marry off, I might introduce one of them to him." Then he'd walked off to the next exam room after tossing her a knowing look, as though he could tell the man had piqued Grace's curiosity.

"Grace! Tell me again about the cowboy," Cindy demanded, bringing Grace's thoughts back to the moment as she drove away from the hospital and headed toward their apartment. She would have driven by the grocery store so they wouldn't have to go tomorrow, but she hated the thought of being seen in her current state with smelly, stained attire.

"There isn't much to tell. He came in for a checkup, called me young, incompetent, and impertinent, and then when I tried to help him put his shirt back on, he flipped his lid. He didn't even finish dressing before he marched out. Just grabbed his hat and left. Hmph! From reading his chart, I know he's only a year older than I am. How dare he insinuate I'm too young and unskilled to do my job properly?"

"Yes. How dare he?" Cindy gave her a long, studying look. "What did he look like? Homely? Dirty? Smelled like horses and cows?"

Grace shook her head, but her mouth engaged before her brain could tell it to stop. "No. He was a real cutie. Blond hair. Blue eyes. Six full feet of muscle and tanned skin. Broad shoulders."

"I see. A real dog, huh?" Cindy waggled her eyebrows in an exaggerated fashion, making Grace laugh.

"You nut. Okay, maybe he was good-looking. Maybe he was strong and fit. And maybe, if he weren't such a jerk, he would be someone I might consider dating."

"And there it is. The real reason you are miffed." Cindy pointed an accusing finger at Grace as she pulled into the apartment's parking lot.

Grace scowled at her. "What are you talking about? I'm upset because he said things about me that aren't true and acted like a genuine dope."

"It's not because he's a hunky cowboy who caught your eye but insulted you in the process?"

A disdainful scoff burst out of Grace as she parked the car. "You've lost your mind, my friend. Come on. I just want to take a shower, eat dinner, and forget about work until Monday."

"Fine by me. How long do you think it will take Jared to get your box?" Cindy asked as they got out and headed into the building.

Grace cast her friend a narrowed look over her shoulder as she checked for mail. "What's going on between you and my brother?"

"Nothing!" Cindy's face turned a deep shade of red, but she feigned innocence as she retrieved her mail. She squealed and clasped a letter to her chest, then raced for the stairs with Grace hot on her heels.

"If that's from Jared, you have to at least let me know he's okay."

"Of course," Cindy said, beaming as they jogged up the stairs and down the hall to their apartment.

By the time Monday morning had rolled around, Grace was even more upset with Sergeant Levi Gibson. How dare he assume that because she was young, she didn't know what she was doing? Even crabby, hard-to-please Dr. Robinson had given her a glowing evaluation last month.

The next time Levi came in for an appointment, she'd make sure Nurse Wells was the one assigned to him. Doubtless, he wouldn't appreciate the pinch-faced older woman's brash commentary or her less-than-gentle touch. Typically, the doctors sicced her on uncooperative patients who'd exceeded the limits of patience with the rest of the nursing staff.

Indignant, and justifiably so, Grace felt the gray clouds overhead matched her attitude as she and Cindy walked out of the apartment building and over to her car.

"Wasn't it a lovely weekend?" Cindy asked, setting her purse and the brown bag holding her lunch on the floor by her feet.

"Lovely? Are you kidding? I spent what felt like hours scrubbing every spot and stain out of my uniforms, doing load after load of laundry, then polishing my work shoes. We ran errands all afternoon Saturday and spent Sunday morning at church. Yesterday afternoon while you wrote my brother a lovey-dovey letter, I baked cookies and bread, and then we made the casseroles we can warm up this week instead of having to cook every night. What, exactly, was lovely about any of that?"

Cindy grinned. "Woke up on the wrong side of the bed this morning, did we?"

"No!" Grace said tersely, feeling her shoulders bunch with tension and inch upward toward her ears. She relaxed them and tried to let go of the residual anger from her encounter with Levi Gibson that had put her in such a grumpy mood. If she didn't release it, she'd be in a snit all day, which wouldn't bode well for her or anyone else.

She released a sigh and glanced at her friend. "I'm sorry. It's just …" Grace had no idea how to explain what she was feeling when she couldn't begin to understand it herself.

Instead of trying, she turned up the radio as the Carpenters sang about rainy days and Mondays. She could relate as big drops of rain began falling from the sky, marring the dust on her windshield.

The windshield wipers could hardly keep up with the deluge as she turned them on high, wishing she'd made time to wash her car over the weekend.

When she reached the hospital, she drove close to the door of the administration building and stopped.

"No use in both of us getting all wet. Have a great day," she said to her friend and waved her inside, then drove over to the staff parking area. She wished she had an umbrella with her, but the need for one was so infrequent this time of year she'd taken it out along with the ice scraper she used in the winter and stored them in the trunk. By the time she dug it out, she'd be soaked through. Good thing she had a spare uniform inside.

With one last glance around the car to see if she had anything she could use to reach the door without getting drenched, she grabbed her purse and lunch, hopped out of the car, and gasped as the cold rain pinged off her skin. She'd only taken a step when the rain suddenly stopped.

More accurately, the rain had been blocked by an umbrella that appeared above her head. She looked up into the face of none other than the man who had tormented her thoughts all weekend.

"Sergeant Gibson?" she asked, wondering if he'd come back to further insult her. If that were the case, he surely wouldn't be holding an umbrella so solicitously over her to keep off the rain.

"Morning, ma'am." He nodded at her, not quite grinning, but certainly not as sour-faced as he'd been when he'd stormed out of the office on Friday. "Let's get you inside."

Grace certainly wasn't going to argue with him. Not when his presence meant she wouldn't be completely drenched by the time she reached the door.

With long, hurried steps, they raced to the hospital's main entrance. Levi paused just outside the door. "Would you mind waiting a minute, Nurse Marshall?"

"I'll wait in the lobby," she said, wondering what he intended. Rather than stand outside in the cool, damp air watching him, she stepped into the lobby and checked to make sure her stockings and shoes looked presentable. A quick wipe with a tissue remedied the few splotches on her shoes. She straightened in time to see Levi sprinting through the rain with a vase of flowers.

His cowboy hat had kept his head dry, but Grace was sure she could wring water out of his shirt when he stepped inside. A vision of him shirtless made warmth sear her cheeks as he walked over to her and held out the vase.

"Here," he said, holding it out to her.

She stared at the vase brimming with fragrant lilacs, white tulips, and pink peonies. The arrangement was stunning, but she had no idea why he'd bring it to her.

Hesitantly, she reached out for the vase. "What's this?"

"An apology," he said, removing his hat as she took the vase from him.

She held the vase against her mid-section, longing to bury her nose in the divine lilacs. She'd always loved the scent of them when they bloomed in the spring. On their dairy farm, they had several old bushes that bloomed along the back fence. She'd missed them since she'd moved to Boise. The only chance she got to smell flowers now was while walking in the park, or when one of her fellow nurses received them as a gift.

"An apology?" she asked, giving the cute cowboy a curious glance.

"For Friday. I was rude, and I'm sorry. It wasn't anything you did," he admitted, appearing both nervous and repentant.

She ignored the way he'd shoved his left hand into the front pocket of his jeans to hide his injury. His right hand clenched his hat, as though he was anxious. Uncertain.

"Do you really think I'm too young, incompetent, and impertinent to be a nurse?" she asked, keeping her expression unreadable, but she shifted her posture, cocking one hip defiantly.

A slow grin spread across his face as he watched her, appearing to keenly observe her every move. His head shook from side to side. "No, ma'am. I think you are more than qualified to do your job, and you were not impertinent. I'm truly sorry for the way I behaved when I was here. The way I acted was unnecessary and unkind, and it bugged me all weekend that I'd been that way with you. Truly, I'm sorry."

"You're forgiven," Grace said, grinning at him and surrendering to her need to sniff the blooms. She closed her eyes to better savor the fragrance, then opened them to find Levi watching her. "I love lilacs."

His grin broadened. "We have a bunch of them at the farm just starting to bloom. The tulips were on the north side of the house, or they'd likely be gone for the season."

"It's a magnificent bouquet. Do you need the vase back?" she asked.

"No. Ma has dozens of them. She gets the credit for arranging the flowers, though. She said to tell you that she did a better job of raising me than you might have previously considered and to please not hold my behavior against her."

"I did have a few thoughts about that this weekend." Grace smiled and hugged the vase a little tighter. "I do thank you, Sergeant Gibson, for these lovely blooms, but I should get to work."

"I didn't mean to keep you. I just wanted to apologize and ask for your forgiveness."

"You are forgiven."

"Thank you," he said, taking a step back toward the door.

Grace had never, not once in her life, considered asking a guy on a date, but a sense of panic welled in her at the thought of not seeing Levi again soon.

The words spilled out of her, leaving her unable to stuff them back into her mouth. "Are you busy next Saturday?" she heard herself ask.

Levi appeared as shocked by the question as Grace felt.

"No. Not really. Did you have something in mind?" he asked, sounding hesitant, as though he expected her to make fun of him or something equally preposterous.

"Would you have any interest in going to the movies?"

A smile broke across Levi's face that was nothing short of dazzling. "I'd like that, Nurse Marshall, but only on two conditions."

What had she done!

She'd asked out a man, which boggled her mind, and that man had infuriated her the first time they'd met. Other than Dr. O'Brien's comment in passing, she knew nothing about Levi Gibson beyond the fact that he was good-looking and seemed sweet, now that he wasn't muttering insults and glowering at her in the exam room.

Maybe it wouldn't be so bad to go to the movies with him. It would certainly be better than her usual Saturday evening activities of watching whatever was on television with Cindy or reading.

While she pondered the possibilities, her thoughts latched onto what he said. Conditions. He would only go out with her on two conditions. If they involved something nefarious, she would call hospital security on him.

"And those conditions are?" she asked, fearful of how he might respond.

He took a step closer to her, and she could practically see his confidence begin to blossom. "Condition one is you'll agree to have dinner with me either before or after the movie."

She nodded, feeling somewhat relieved. Dinner was innocent, practical, and a normal thing one would do on a date. "That's agreeable."

"Condition two," he said, smiling again in that charming way that made her stomach flutter. "Is that you'll tell me your name and give me your phone number in case something happens between now and then and one of us needs to cancel."

Grace had no intention of canceling. Not when the handsome cowboy had charmed her with an umbrella, lilacs, and a sincere apology. However, maybe he had no interest in seeing her again and would call Friday afternoon to let her know he couldn't make it.

Perhaps she was reading far more into the situation than was warranted.

"Come over here," she said, leading the way to the receptionist's desk. Grace set down the flowers, wrote out her name and phone number on a slip of paper, and handed it to him, then held out the pen and a notepad to him.

He shook his head. "You write it. It will look like a drunken chicken danced in an inkwell if I try."

She barely held back a giggle as she wrote his name and the phone number to both his home and his parents' home on a piece of paper, tucking it in her purse.

"Would you like me to pick you up at your place or meet somewhere?" Levi asked as he took a step back from the desk.

She liked that he'd offered to meet somewhere, making her feel that he'd put her in control of the dating parameters.

"Call me Friday evening, and we'll figure out the details," she said with a warm smile, then lifted her hand in a wave as he nodded and left.

She waited until he dashed back across the parking lot out of view to glance at the receptionist.

The woman cocked a penciled-on eyebrow at her. "He's cute and sweet."

"He sure seems to be," Grace agreed, then glanced down at the vase. "Would you mind if I leave these here today? You know how the doctors are about flowers upsetting the patients in our office."

"I don't mind at all having these beauties to keep me company all day," the receptionist grinned as she sniffed the lilacs. "Makes me think of my grandma."

"Me too!" Grace smiled at the woman and rushed to clock in on time. She could hardly wait for the day to end so she could tell Cindy that the cowboy who had upset her whole weekend had miraculously turned out not to be a big jerk after all.

Levi wiped his damp palms on the legs of his jeans, took a deep breath, and walked into the apartment building where Grace said she lived.

Grace Marshall.

Now that he knew her name, Levi would never forget it. Or her.

He'd spent all last weekend feeling guilty and terrible about the way he'd left the hospital in a foul mood and for the things he'd said under his breath about Grace. Even as he'd muttered them, he knew they weren't true. Her presence had unsettled him so much he'd felt completely unlike himself.

It wasn't until he'd arrived back at the farm with the parts his dad had ordered and the groceries his mom had wanted that he had acknowledged he'd acted like a blustering blockhead. Levi might no longer be full of laughter and fun, but he wasn't rude or condescending. It disturbed him more than he cared to admit that he'd acted that way to a woman who'd just wanted to help him.

After church on Sunday, as he joined his parents for lunch at their house, he brought up what had happened. His mother had lectured him for twenty minutes on minding his manners while his father had given him several you-know-better-than-that looks that made Levi feel like he was nine years old.

When he'd asked if they thought he should apologize, his father nodded while his mother spent another twenty minutes discussing, mostly with herself, all the appropriate ways he could offer a sincere apology.

The flowers she suggested seemed like the simplest thing to do. His mother had helped him choose the blooms and arranged them on Sunday evening. The thought of taking the flowers up to the doctor's office and asking for Nurse Marshall had made Levi feel sick to his stomach, so he had decided he'd drive to the hospital early Monday morning and wait for her arrival. His patience had paid off. He'd watched Grace pull up in a sporty teal blue Impala that looked like it would be a blast to drive. It wasn't the vehicle he'd pictured her owning, but she appeared both comfortable and confident behind the wheel.

Before she could get out of the car, he'd grabbed the umbrella his mother had insisted he take with him because it looked like rain—was

Stella Gibson *ever* wrong?—and rushed over to hold it for Grace as she got out of the car.

She looked utterly taken aback to see him. For the briefest moment, he'd seen questions in her eyes, but she'd allowed him to hold the umbrella for her as they rushed to the hospital's main entrance, then she'd waited inside while he retrieved the flowers.

She'd been open to accepting his apology, then had shocked him by asking if he was busy tonight.

Honestly, if she hadn't offered the invitation, Levi wouldn't have worked up the courage to ask her on a date. Not after he'd insulted her and acted like a petulant child in the exam room.

Despite his embarrassment over his behavior, he'd been eager to see her again.

When he'd phoned last night to see what time she'd like to get together, she'd suggested he pick her up at her apartment and given him directions. They'd made plans to eat dinner first, then go to the movies.

Levi made his way up the stairs to the second floor of the apartment building, then found the apartment door with her number and knocked twice on the portal.

Out of habit, he shoved his left hand into his front jeans pocket, then stepped back, hearing voices inside just before the door swung open.

The woman smiling at him in welcome looked nothing like the nurse he'd first encountered. The stark white of her uniform and the severity of the bun she wore at the back of her head did little to diminish her attractiveness.

Yet, seeing her now, she appeared incredibly feminine and lovely with her hair flowing in thick waves around her, wearing a floral dress in shades of teal blue and white. Instead of her sensible and somewhat ugly, nurse's shoes, she had on a pair of wedge sandals that added a few inches to her already tall height.

If Levi hadn't left his cowboy hat at home, he might have swept it off his head and bowed to her in greeting. As it was, he couldn't hold back a satisfied smile at seeing her. He drew in a breath and found his senses ensnared by her tropical fragrance.

Man, did she smell good.

Levi took a second whiff before he yanked his thoughts together and forced his stiff posture to relax.

"Hi, Grace. I hope I'm not too early. I wasn't sure how long it would take me to get here."

"From Star, right?" she asked, stepping back so he could enter the apartment.

The living room was tidy and smelled like cookies, making him wonder if Grace had been baking that afternoon. He liked the eclectic mix of furniture and the fact that the walls and décor weren't bright, gaudy colors, but subtle and subdued.

"You have a nice place here," he said as his eyes roved around the room, landing on a female who stood in the doorway to the kitchen. She was cute, in a pair of jeans with the cuffs rolled up and a cotton top, with her blonde hair pulled into a ponytail tied with a yellow ribbon.

"This is my roommate and best friend, Cindy Milton. Cindy, meet Levi Gibson."

Levi held out a hand and met the girl halfway across the living room. She shook his hand with enough enthusiasm that it made him grin, then she gave him a teasing wink and tipped her head toward Grace.

"Grace has been looking forward to seeing you all week. I hope the two of you have a great time."

Levi bit his cheek to hold back a laugh at the furious frown Grace tossed to Cindy. Her cheeks had turned a bright shade of pink, betraying the humiliation she felt at the comment. He was grateful to Cindy, though, for making it known he wasn't the only one who'd been anticipating his date with Grace this evening.

"What will you do this evening, Miss Milton?" Levi asked as Grace gathered her purse and dropped in a set of keys.

"Nothing. I plan to enjoy every second of it," she said with a silly grin. "Call me Cindy."

"Then I hope you'll call me Levi. Have a nice evening."

"You two enjoy yourselves," Cindy said, practically shoving Grace out the door.

Grace cast one more warning look at her friend, then stepped into the hallway, leading the way to the stairs. Levi walked a few steps behind her, enjoying the way her hair and hips swayed as she walked down the steps and across the lobby.

He hurried to push open the door and hold it for her. Another whiff of her decadent fragrance nearly scrambled his thoughts as she passed by him. How could something as simple as her perfume make him long for sandy beaches and a fruity drink in his hand? He was the last person anyone would find lounging on a beach or drinking out of a coconut. In fact, the vision of him doing such a thing almost made him chuckle as he followed Grace outside and pointed to his pickup, which he'd taken time to wash earlier that afternoon. He'd wiped down the inside until it was spotless and the glass in the windows sparkled.

Grace gave him a gracious nod as he opened the pickup door for her. She didn't need his assistance to slide onto the seat, but he sure wanted to reach out and touch her hand, just to make sure she was real and not a dream he'd been lost in since Monday.

It had been hard to concentrate on farmwork or work at his house, with an image of Grace's smile firmly planted in his mind.

His mother had nagged him incessantly about what he planned to wear and where he planned to take Grace and then offered endless advice about how to make a good impression on her, all of which he ignored. A suit, something he generally only donned for weddings or funerals, wasn't appropriate for a casual dinner and a movie, no matter how much his mother argued otherwise.

Levi had polished his best pair of boots, bought a new pair of jeans and washed them three times so they wouldn't be too stiff to wear, and then relented and let his mother press every last wrinkle out of one of his favorite shirts. She wouldn't let him leave without a tie on, which looked absurd and out of place with the western shirt. As soon as he drove down the driveway, he yanked it off and stuffed it into the jockey box.

Now, seeing Grace look so lovely and sophisticated in her dress, he wondered if he should have worn something else.

"You look quite handsome, kind sir," Grace said as she settled her skirt around her on the seat.

He smiled at her. "You look breathtaking, Grace," he said, then closed the pickup door.

A blush burned up his neck and over his cheeks as he walked around the pickup and got behind the wheel. Was that a good thing to say? Or a dumb thing? He was so out of practice when it came to dating, he felt like he was starting all over again. His stomach was tied in knots, his palms might start dripping sweat at any moment, and he fought the urge to create a flimsy excuse to race back home.

Grace was the first girl who'd caught his interest in a long time. He'd be an idiot and a fool to waste this opportunity to get to spend time with her, to get to know her better.

"It's warm today, isn't it?" she asked, rolling down the window and letting the fresh air blow into the cab as he pulled out of the apartment parking lot and drove up the street.

As he drove, the breeze carried that tropical scent to his nose again. Her fragrance tantalized him to the point he wanted to draw in great lungfuls of it, but he somehow refrained.

"It is warm," he eventually agreed, realizing he'd been staring at her instead of replying. How long of a pause between a question and answer was considered acceptable before it moved into the territory of being completely lame? He was fairly certain he'd reached birdbrain status when he finally yanked his thoughts together. "I heard about a new place that opened a few months ago. Would you like to try it for dinner, or do you have anything in mind?"

"I'm willing to try somewhere new. I'm not hard to please when it comes to food. As long as it tastes good, I'm happy with it."

"Good to know," he said, turning onto a side street, then glancing over at Grace. She was looking out the window, studying the passing scenery with her profile to him, appearing at ease. He could envision dozens of trips with her, going out to eat or to the movies, off on a fun adventure. Would a baby or two fit on the seat between them?

Slow that horse down, hoss, he admonished himself. This was only their first date. He didn't need to start planning a future that would likely never happen, especially if he didn't get his act together.

"What about you?" she asked as he slowed and pulled into the parking lot at the new diner. Orange and yellow plaid curtains hung in the windows, and a big sign advertised it was now open for business. A neon coffee cup sign stood over the top of the building.

"What about me?" he asked as he eyed a parking spot and pulled into it.

"What do you like to eat, or what won't you eat?"

He shrugged. "I'm not terribly picky, but I am no longer fond of rice, and I detest any kind of meat that comes in a can, especially if it's cold."

She gave him a studying glance, then nodded in understanding. "So, no Chinese food for you."

"Not if there is any other option available." He grinned and got out of the pickup, then hurried around to open her door for her. When he held out his hand, she took it and gave it a light squeeze, causing an electrical current to dance up his arm. It was almost like grabbing a hot fence wire, but instead of experiencing the urge to release it and jump back, he never wanted to let go.

He glanced down at her delicate, long fingers and then up to her face that was near enough to his he could have easily leaned forward and kissed her. Would her lips taste as honeyed as he imagined? Or would she slap him so hard that his ears would still be ringing a week from now?

Unwilling to find out, he moved back and shut the pickup door with his elbow.

"Is your pickup new?" she asked as they walked across the parking lot. He'd felt encouraged when she held onto his hand instead of moving away from him.

"I've had it about a month. I'd planned to buy a new pickup before I enlisted, but I'm glad I waited. This one is just what I was looking for."

She smiled at him as he released her hand and opened the restaurant's door, holding it for her to precede him. "It's great, Levi. The design on the seats and the door panels is so striking."

The acanthus scrolls embossed on the door panels and into the white leather seat gave the vehicle a western edge that he liked. His mother had told him the design was perfect to impress a girl, if he ever caught one.

Not that he'd been fishing for one, or even had his pole in the water recently, but if he had been, Grace Marshall was exactly the kind of girl he'd want to catch.

"Table for two?" a hostess asked, then picked up menus and led them to a booth in the corner without giving him a chance to reply.

Levi waited until Grace slid into the booth to take a seat facing both her and the door. He knew he was safe, but sometimes he just felt a need to be able to keep the exit in his line of sight. With nerves bubbling in his stomach and fear stabbing at him over doing or saying something he shouldn't, the stress of the evening was about to overwhelm his ability to remain calm and rational.

When their waitress set two glasses of ice water in front of them, Levi drained half his glass and then gave the waitress a sheepish look as she placed napkins and silverware on the table.

"Anything besides water to drink?" she asked, looking at him and then Grace.

"I'd like a lemonade, please," Grace said, smiling at the middle-aged woman.

"Do you have sweet tea?" Levi asked without glancing at the menu.

"Is there any other kind?" the woman asked with a cheeky grin.

He smiled. "No, ma'am."

"I'll bring your drinks and a pitcher of water while you decide what to order. The special tonight is meatloaf or beef stew. We also serve breakfast all day."

Grace immediately flipped over the menu to the back and perused the breakfast offerings. Levi opened his menu and decided on the turkey dinner. He could get all the good, grass-fed beef he wanted at home, but they only had turkey at Thanksgiving.

"Anything look good?" he asked after he closed the menu and scooted it over to the edge of the table.

"Everything," she looked up with a happy smile. "I love breakfast. It's my favorite meal. If Cindy wouldn't complain, I'd probably make breakfast for dinner every time it was my turn to cook."

"You take turns cooking?" he asked, wondering if Grace was a good cook, not that it mattered. Even his poor attempts at cooking tasted like fine cuisine compared to what he'd eaten in Vietnam.

"We do. We alternate every other night. That way, neither of us is stuck doing all the cooking, although most of the time, we end up working together. A few nights a week, we try to cook enough of something to have plenty of leftovers, and we generally do some baking on the weekends so we don't have to do it the rest of the week."

"Sounds like you have a system that works." He tried to think of something witty or at least halfway intelligent to say, but nothing came to him. Instead, he downed the rest of the water in his glass, then looked around, hoping the waitress would quickly return.

"What about you? Do you cook?" Grace asked as she placed her menu on top of his and leaned back in the booth.

"Only under duress. I can make toast and eggs without setting anything on fire, and I'm pretty handy with my dad's barbecue grill. I can cook a good steak or burger on it."

"That's neat. My folks haven't yet decided they should get a barbecue, but Cindy's dad makes the best frankfurters on his."

The waitress arrived with their drinks and took their orders before she filled Levi's water glass and left the pitcher on the table.

"Does your family live nearby?" Levi asked Grace once they were alone, grateful to have finally landed on a topic that might involve more than one or two questions and could carry them through at least a few minutes of conversation.

Grace shook her head, causing the hair surrounding her face to sway enticingly. She tossed her hair back over her shoulders and took a sip of her water before she answered. "They live in Holiday, Oregon."

Levi riffled through his brain, trying to recall if he'd ever heard of Holiday. He thought it was maybe up in the mountains but wasn't entirely certain. "Is it near Pendleton?"

"No, not quite that far. It's northeast of Baker City. About an hour from there up in the mountains. The air there is so crisp and fresh. To me, it always smells like Christmas."

He smiled. "Does your family work in the timber industry?"

"No. We have a dairy. Cindy's folks own a dry goods store, with clothing and household goods, fabric, that sort of thing."

"I see. Tell me more about the dairy. How many head do your parents milk?"

Grace talked about their dairy operation with both knowledge and skill, making him think she'd helped milk more than her share of cows. He tried to picture her out in a barn dodging a manure-coated tail but just couldn't quite make it take shape in his mind. Not when she looked like she could have walked right out of a fashion magazine.

"So, you have three brothers?" Levi asked, pulling that tidbit of information from something she'd mentioned about milking with her siblings.

"Yes. Micah is the oldest. He'll take over the dairy someday. He loves the farm and would never consider leaving. Jared is two years older than me, and he's currently in Vietnam. Last I heard, he was doing okay, but he's looking forward to coming home in August. Jason is almost five years younger than me, and he's taking agriculture-focused business classes at Oregon State University in Corvallis. He has one more year before he graduates. His hope is to get a job with Sinclair Industries and build a career working for the company. None of them are married, and my mother is beginning to fear she's failed in raising us, me most of all since I chose a career over becoming a housewife right out of school."

He chuckled. "I'm pretty sure my mom thinks the same thing. What about your dad?"

Grace grinned. "I'm his favorite, but don't tell the others. Dad supports and encourages me, as well as my brothers. He's probably a little harder on Jason because he's the baby, but Mom has spoiled him until he's almost rotten. In fact, Dad just sent me the coolest gift the other day."

"Really? What was it?"

"A pistol."

Unable to hide his shock, his eyes widened, and Grace smirked, aware she'd caught him off guard.

"That wasn't what you expected, was it?" she asked.

Before he could reply, the waitress returned with their meals. After she set their plates in front of them and placed a pitcher of syrup on the table to go with Grace's French toast, she fisted her hands on her ample hips and looked from Levi to Grace. "Anything else for you kids?"

Levi looked at Grace, who gave a slight shake of her head. He smiled at the waitress and nodded politely. "Thank you. This all looks great."

"Enjoy!" the woman bustled off, leaving them to their meals.

Levi surveyed the tender slices of turkey, the mound of potatoes and gravy, another mound of sage-scented dressing, a scoop of steamed carrots and peas, and a spoonful of cranberry sauce on his plate and concluded he'd made a great choice with his meal. He looked over to see Grace slathering warm butter across her French toast, then pouring syrup over the top. She had a thick slice of smoky ham, crispy hash browns, and a fried egg on her plate, along with a tiny fruit cup that held two strawberries and half a dozen green grapes.

When Grace bowed her head, Levi reached across the table and took her hand in his. Startled, she looked up at him, but he bowed his head and offered a quiet blessing on their meal that only the two of them could hear.

"Amen," she said, then smiled at him. "Thanks for that. Might I assume you attend a church?"

"Every Sunday as long as I can remember unless I was gone or sick. I'm pretty sure the fifth pew on the left side at the Star Community Church has a permanent imprint of our backsides."

Grace laughed softly. "That sounds like us at home. We always sit in the seventh pew on the right side. My spot is between Daddy and Micah."

He liked the way she called her father "Daddy" and spoke of her family with such fondness. It gave him insight into her character to know she loved her family, and the fact that she'd grown up in a small town on a farm didn't hurt anything either.

Levi had dated a number of girls in the past, several of whom lived in town, and none of them had enjoyed coming out to the farm. Once they found out he had no inclination to move into Boise, it meant the end to all but one of those relationships. The only girl who hadn't cared he was a farmer took quite an exception to his being a soldier.

Regardless, Grace, a girl who'd been raised in the country, would understand how much Levi needed the open spaces, fresh air, and the dirt beneath his feet. At least, he hoped she would, assuming he didn't botch their first date so badly that she'd never speak to him again.

He took a few bites of his meal, then looked to Grace. "You started to tell me about a pistol your dad sent to you. What is it? A Colt?"

"Well, it looks like a Colt, but it has pink mother-of-pearl grips. It once belonged to Annie Oakley."

Levi's eyes widened in surprise again. "That is amazing. Where did he find it?"

"He was at a dairy meeting in Salem and found it in a junk store, which is so out of character for Dad to go into a place like that. Anyway, the sales clerk told him the gun had belonged to an actress of whom Dad is quite fond. She's old now, but back in the day, she was popular. I think he bought it because the actress might have owned it at one time but also because it's so pretty."

Levi watched as Grace took a dainty bite of her French toast. Before he lost his nerve, he decided to ask the question darting around in his mind like a kernel of popcorn hopping around in a hot skillet.

"If you haven't shot it yet and would like to try hitting some targets, you could come out to my place next weekend."

"For real?" Grace dabbed at her mouth with her napkin and gave him an earnest look of interest. "You wouldn't mind?"

"Not at all. I'd like to see this pink pistol of yours." He leaned a little closer and lowered his voice, as though he were about to reveal a secret. "But don't let my mother see it. She loves the color pink and might just talk you out of it."

"No," she said, cutting a piece of her ham. "I don't think I could part with it. Not now, anyway."

Levi listened as she explained about her great-grandpa's cousin once having it in her possession and was awed to think the woman had once worked in a mine, setting dynamite blasts.

"Wow, Grace. Did Rena make it into any history books for doing work so unusual for a woman at the time?"

"Not that I'm aware of, but she should have been. I never met her, but she's something of a legend in my family."

"I could easily imagine she would be." He took a drink of tea, then looked at Grace again. "Any other fascinating characters in your family tree?"

Grace laughed again. "No. We're a pretty boring, run-of-the-mill bunch of simple country folk."

The look he leveled across the table held disbelief. "If you tell me you're only a step beyond hillbillies, I'll know you're fibbing. No one who looks and acts like you could ever be considered simple country folk."

She blushed and fell silent, and he wondered if he'd said more than he should have. When she gazed at him from beneath her crazy-long eyelashes, he decided maybe his foot wasn't lodged in his mouth along with his last bite of turkey.

Once the waitress returned to remove their plates and they both declined dessert, Levi excused himself to the restroom. Two glasses of water and one of iced tea had caught up with him. He returned to the table, and Grace politely excused herself to powder her nose. Levi paid their bill while she was gone and stood when she returned, cupping her elbow as they made their way to the door. He used his left shoulder to push the door open and hold it as Grace walked outside, then took her hand in his, hoping she wouldn't pull away.

Inordinately gratified when she moved a step closer, he did his best to hide his smile. "Is there any movie, in particular, you'd like to see?"

"Well, there is one I thought looked good, but I don't know if that's your kind of thing," she said as he opened the pickup door and waited until she had her skirt settled around her on the seat to shut it.

He jogged around the pickup and slid behind the wheel. "I'm fine with whatever. Just tell me where it's playing, and that's where we'll go."

"The newspaper listing said it was still playing at the downtown theater. You know, the one with the Egyptian theme."

He grinned and put the pickup in reverse, backing out of the parking space. "I haven't been there in years. It'll be fun to see that old place again. Didn't it originally open in the twenties?"

"I think I read that somewhere," she said, sounding uncertain.

He'd forgotten she hadn't grown up in the area because, for reasons he couldn't begin to explain, it felt like he'd known her forever.

It didn't take long to drive downtown and find a parking space across the street from the theater. The restaurants and bars seemed busy, as well as the hotels in the area.

As they crossed the street, Levi held out his arm to Grace, and she wrapped her hand around it, moving closer to him with a smile.

After purchasing two movie tickets, they bypassed the concession stand and made their way into the theater. Grace claimed she couldn't possibly hold another bite after their filling dinner.

Levi allowed Grace to choose the seats, grateful she selected two at the end of the row at the very back where he could sit with his back to the wall. She smiled as he took a seat beside her and stretched out his legs in the aisle.

"Do you go to the movies often?" he asked quietly as they waited for the movie to begin, wondering if he should have at least bought a small box of popcorn for them to munch on during the show.

"Not often. Cindy and I went in January, I think, to a Saturday matinee. We got two tickets for the price of one." Grace leaned toward him and lowered her voice. "By the time you buy tickets and snacks, it can get expensive."

"It can, but then again, there isn't any other popcorn quite like the overly salty, way too greasy stuff you can find at a movie theater."

She laughed softly. "You are correct on that point."

"I'll go get some if you like," Levi offered, starting to rise from his seat.

"No. I'm fine, Levi. Truly. My dinner was delicious, and I'm full. Maybe we can get dessert after the movie. My treat."

There was no way he'd allow her to pay for dessert, but he was thrilled she wanted to spend more time together after the movie. Perhaps that meant he hadn't completely forgotten the basics of dating or lost what little skill he'd previously possessed in charming a girl.

The lights dimmed, and the movie started. Levi had hoped and prayed that sitting in the dark surrounded by strangers wouldn't trigger his flight-or-fight response, but with Grace's entrancing fragrance floating around him and her warmth penetrating his side, he felt at ease.

For the next hour and a half, he found himself watching the antics of two little boys trying to train a bird dog that seemed completely untrainable. The end was, as Levi expected, heartwarming, and when the lights came back on, he noticed Grace dabbing at her tears with a tissue.

"Sorry. Sappy movies and stories get to me," she said, wiping away one errant tear, then releasing a long breath. "I hope you didn't mind the movie. It wasn't exactly a car chase or blowing something up or whatever it is you like. Those are generally the story lines my brothers prefer."

Levi shrugged. "I'm more of a guy who enjoys a good western."

She grinned at him. "That should have been obvious from the boots and the cowboy hat you generally wear. We never got around to talking about you earlier. Do you do ranch work for a living?"

"Nope. I'm a farmer."

Her gaze widened as they stood and waited for the crowd to thin so they could walk down the aisle and out of the theater.

"You're a farmer?" she asked, sounding somewhat incredulous.

"Didn't I mention that?" Levi asked, placing his hand on Grace's back as they moved into the theater's lobby.

"No, you did not. I just assumed with the cowboy clothes that …" She snapped her mouth shut, waited until they were outside in the cool evening air, then turned to him. "What exactly type of farmer are you?"

"Potatoes, mostly, although we put about fifteen percent of our acreage into sugar beets ten years ago."

A frown creased her forehead. "Gibson. Potatoes. Your family farm is Gibson & Son?"

Levi nodded, surprised she'd heard of them. Granted, their potatoes were sold in grocery stores all around the area, but most people paid no mind to the name printed on the bags.

"And you're the son part of that?" she asked as Levi took her hand, and they hurried across the street to his pickup.

"Guilty," he said with a grin, opening the door and offering a hand that she took as she climbed in, appearing to be deep in thought. He jogged around the pickup, slid behind the wheel, closed the floor vent he'd left open, and looked at Grace.

She stared at him as though he'd sprouted horns on top of his head. Discomfited by her direct gaze, he searched for a distraction.

"Would you still like dessert?" he asked, wondering why she seemed almost perturbed by the fact that he was a farmer, not a cowboy. Just because shirts with snaps were easier for him to manage, and he preferred cowboy boots to other forms of footwear shouldn't mean anything. Should it?

"Dessert," she repeated, then nodded once.

"Pie? Ice cream? Cake?" Levi asked.

"Sure," she said, then looked out the window as though lost in thought.

Her reaction to his chosen path in life made it seem as though she was disappointed that he wasn't a real cowboy. He did have horses and enjoyed riding, and there were beef cattle they raised on the farm for their own use, but he'd never wanted to rope and ride the range as his choice of career. Levi had always felt happiest working the land that had been in his family since wagons rolled through on the Oregon Trail.

Levi drove to a restaurant he'd eaten at numerous times over the years and guided her inside to a booth in the back.

It wasn't until he'd ordered a slice of peach pie with ice cream and Grace had chosen a piece of lemon meringue pie that she looked to him again, appearing contrite for her silence.

"I'm sorry, Levi. The realization I'd made erroneous assumptions based solely on your attire left me a little rattled. I'm sorry. My brothers all dress similar to you when they go to town, so I don't know why I just assumed you were a cowboy. I'd like to hear more about your farm. It's been in your family for a while, hasn't it? I think I read something about it in the newspaper last spring."

He nodded. "I'm the fourth generation to live there. My grandparents had two boys, and they split the work and the farm when my grandparents passed. Then my uncle decided he wanted to try his own thing, so Pop bought his share, and he moved his family up to Pasco, Washington, nine years ago."

"The house you mentioned to Dr. O'Brien, is that on the farm?"

Levi was impressed she'd recalled that comment from his appointment last week. "Yep. It was my uncle's house. It's been empty all this time, but thanks to my mother's ability to smother me nearly to death, I moved into it not long after I returned home. My dad helped me over the winter months to complete some of the bigger projects. Right now, I'm doing some finishing work in my spare time. I really need to buy furniture and wrap things up before my mother insists on helping me."

Grace laughed. "She sounds like she really cares about you."

"She does. So does Pop. Sometimes I wish I had nine siblings so Ma had more than just me to dote on and fuss over."

"Does she have any hobbies?" Grace asked, stirring a spoon of sugar into the hot tea the waitress brought to her while Levi took a drink of the milk he'd ordered.

He swallowed. "You mean in addition to trying to run my life and my dad's? Not really."

Grace lifted an eyebrow and continued stirring her tea to cool it enough to drink. "Maybe you should help her find a few. Then, she might have less time to cluck over her lone chick."

"I'll be sure to tell her you referred to her as a fussy ol' hen."

Aghast, she shook a finger at him. "Levi Gibson! I said no such thing! Don't you dare say that to her. When I meet her, I don't need her to automatically hate me. Mothers tend to dislike the girls their sons date, you know, without making things worse on purpose."

Encouraged by what she'd said, he assumed she intended to go out with him again. He'd thought their evening had gone well, but the fact that Grace mentioned meeting his mother at some point in the future buoyed his spirits.

"Stella Gibson is not your usual mother," Levi said. "She'd think your comment was hilarious, and then she'd give you a long, in-depth list of all my worst habits and character flaws. If you hadn't run off by then, she'd welcome you with open arms and invite you into her inner domain, also known as the kitchen, and insist you bake something together."

"Really? You know all this from past experience?" Grace questioned, tossing him a dubious look as the waitress returned with their slices of pie.

Levi realized he'd said too much. Now he'd have to tell her about Laurie, and he didn't want to. However, the topic would eventually arise if they continued dating, so he might as well get it out in the open now.

"I was engaged before I enlisted. A girl from Meridian named Laurie. We dated almost a year before I proposed, then I enlisted and went off to Vietnam. I'd only been at boot camp a week when she broke things off in a letter. Two months later, she married a guy she'd only known a few days and moved to Twin Falls to open a travel agency with him, or so her father told mine." Levi jabbed his fork into the warm pie. "And that was that."

Grace reached across the table and placed her hand on Levi's wrist. He looked over at her, expecting to see pity or sympathy, but her face was filled with concern while sparks of anger flickered in her eyes.

"I'm sorry she did that to you, Levi. That was a crummy thing to do, especially when you needed to focus on training and preparing for what awaited you over there."

There was no doubt in his mind that Grace would never break off an engagement in a short, terse note and then fail to return an expensive diamond engagement ring.

"I think I knew well before I enlisted that she was going to break up with me, but I didn't want to face it. Her letter just made it all final." Levi took a bite of the pie topped with melting vanilla ice cream, wondering if talking about the girl he'd once planned to marry on his first date qualified him as a first-class dummy.

"Well, I still think it was a lousy thing to do to you. Women like that are a menace."

Levi could have kissed Grace right then for saying what he'd thought the past few years. He wanted nothing more than to lean across the table and press his lips to hers, but he somehow held back from following the impulse.

"What about you?" he asked and forked another bite of pie.

"Was I engaged to a girl named Laurie?" Grace asked with a mischievous grin that melted Levi's heart.

"No," he shook his head, loving that she felt relaxed enough around him to tease. "I just wondered if you'd been engaged or had a special someone in your past."

Grace shook her head. "Nope. Never engaged or even close to engaged. Cindy was, though."

He listened as she talked about her friend's fiancé, a boy they'd both known in high school, his death in Vietnam, and the romance between Cindy and Grace's brother that was blossoming right beneath her nose.

"When did you say your brother will return home?"

"Last I heard, he should return around the first of August. I pray every day he'll soon be back in Holiday where he belongs. Although, if he and Cindy really do have a future together, I could see him moving here."

"Does he have training or a degree in a particular area?" Levi asked, then took a long swig of his milk, draining most of the liquid from the glass.

"He did two years of vocational school and is a certified auto mechanic. He can fix anything that has an engine in it. It shouldn't be hard for him to find work."

"I would think he'd have several job opportunities no matter where he chooses to live." Levi could even ask his dad if he knew anyone in need of a trained mechanic. They could always use someone on the farm with solid mechanic skills. Levi and his dad were both decent mechanics, but on a farm the size of theirs, they often needed extra hands to keep the equipment running.

"Mmm. This pie is so good. Do you want a taste?" Grace held out a bite on her fork for him.

Levi didn't care for lemon, but it was less about the pie and more about Grace being willing to share with him that made him smile and accept the bite.

"Not bad for lemon," he said with a grin, then offered her a sample of the peach.

"Not bad for peach," she said, mimicking him after she'd accepted a taste.

They both laughed and finished their dessert.

Twenty minutes later, Grace held onto his arm as he walked her into her apartment building and up the stairs. They lingered at her door, neither of them ready to call it an evening, but both knowing it was time to end their date.

"I had a great time, Levi. Thank you for dinner and the movie and dessert."

"Thanks for asking me," he said, grinning at her. "It's not every day a beautiful woman invites me out for a fun evening."

She gave him a studying glance. "I bet you get asked out all the time."

"If all the time is the same as never, then sure."

She laughed softly. "Then all the women you know are blind and dumb."

Before he could come up with a reply, she kissed his cheek, opened the apartment door, and closed it quietly behind her.

Levi felt like shouting in victory, but instead, he hustled back down to his pickup and drove home, feeling lighter in spirit than he had in a long, long time.

5

"Are you sure you don't want to come along?" Grace asked as she added a pair of silver hoop earrings to her ears, then studied her reflection in the mirror.

Although the weather had been warm and pleasant the past week, this morning had dawned cool and overcast.

Instead of the sleeveless shirt and shorts she'd intended to wear out to Levi's place for target practice, Grace pulled on a short-sleeved blouse, dark blue jeans, and a long, open cotton sweater with earthy-hued stripes.

Levi had invited her to come any time after one and asked if she'd stay for dinner with his parents. Grace knew meeting his mom and dad was a big step that hinted at commitment. Didn't it?

In truth, she barely knew Levi.

Granted, he'd joined her for lunch at the hospital cafeteria on Tuesday and taken her and Cindy out for burgers after work on Thursday. Even so, their relationship was new, and she wasn't sure she was ready to take the enormous step of meeting his family.

"I think you need to meet his parents without a sidekick." Cindy snapped the piece of gum she was chewing and grinned as she sat sideways in an armchair, feet over one arm, and flipped through the Sears spring catalog. "Besides, you need time alone with Levi to get to know him better." Cindy glanced up at her. "For the record, I think he's handsome, funny, and kind."

"So, you've given him your stamp of approval?"

Cindy grinned and popped a bubble. "The official stamp of approval. Now, go have fun."

Grace slipped on a pair of yellow flats. "I hate to leave you all alone this afternoon and for dinner tonight."

"I'll be fine. I'm perfectly capable of taking care of myself." Cindy set aside the catalog and stood, arms crossed over her chest, head tilted to the side, as she studied Grace. "Your outfit needs something."

Grace turned back to the mirror to critically catalog her reflection. She thought her choices worked together and made her look both fashionable yet traditional. She had a feeling Levi's parents wouldn't be wowed by a girl who showed up in skin-tight bell-bottom pants or a skirt so short it barely hid anything, not that Grace owned either of those things.

"I know just the thing!" Cindy hurried across the hall into her bedroom and returned with a fawn-colored felt hat that had cream lace trim around the band that encircled the crown. "You need this to tie it all together."

Grace started to refuse, but when Cindy settled the hat on her head, she knew her friend was correct. It did finish the outfit and looked nice.

"I'll do my best not to get it dirty."

Cindy shrugged. "I hardly ever wear it. You might as well enjoy it."

Together, they walked into the living room, where Grace picked up the pistol case and her purse, along with an orange Tupperware container she'd filled with cookies for Levi. She wasn't certain what kind he liked, but she'd tried a new pineapple cookie recipe she'd found in a cookbook her mom had given her when she'd first left home. Cindy had deemed the cookies delicious, and Grace thought the one she'd tried had tasted good, so hopefully, Levi would enjoy them.

Grace gave Cindy one last look as her friend opened the door for her. "Are you sure—"

Cindy gave her a playful shove into the hall. "Go! Have fun! I'll be waiting to hear all about your adventures on the farm with your potato-growing cowboy when you return."

"He's not a cowboy," Grace reminded Cindy. When she'd realized Levi was a farmer, not a cowboy, she'd felt an acute sense of disappointment. In her mind, she'd envisioned romantic horseback rides and moonlight serenades with the life she'd imagined he'd led. Since she'd never dated a cowboy, it had seemed quite thrilling.

How childish she'd been, sulking when she'd learned the truth. Besides, she was a farm girl, and there wasn't a single thing wrong with being a farmer. In fact, it was what her father referred to as one of the last honorable professions, tasked with feeding the world.

In retrospect, a farmer was probably more settled and responsible than someone who could perform daring feats aback his trusty steed. Wasn't he? A vision of Levi riding a horse while doing rope tricks flashed into her mind.

Amused by the direction her thoughts had taken, Grace set her things on the seat beside her in the car, drove away from the apartment complex, and followed the directions Levi had given to her Thursday to find the Gibson & Son property just outside of the small town of Star.

It only took her about twenty minutes to reach the pink mailbox that had Gibson painted on the side of it. Grace turned onto the dirt road and recalled Levi mentioning his mother's love of pink. Apparently, that carried all the way out to the mailbox.

She turned at the first road she came to and followed it around tidy fields that had already been planted with this year's potato and beet crops. As nothing but fields continued to surround her, she wondered if she'd read the directions wrong or turned when she should have kept going.

Eventually, she rounded a bend and could see a house up ahead.

When she rolled to a stop in front of a two-story Craftsman house painted a soothing shade of green with cream and dark green trim, she knew she'd found Levi's place. He'd mentioned he'd recently painted it in the original 1920s hues. Grace loved the style of the house and the colors Levi had selected that blended into the landscape. The lawn was green, and several neatly trimmed shrubs surrounded the porch that stretched across the front of the house. Tall maple and oak trees surrounded the yard. She assumed they would be wonderful for providing cooling shade on hot summer days.

She opened the car door and got out, walking around it to retrieve her things. Levi hurried out of the house and down the porch steps. His smile brightened the day even if there wasn't any sunshine peeking through the clouds overhead.

"Hi, stranger," he said, taking the gun case from her and motioning toward the house as she slipped the strap of her purse over her shoulder. "I'm glad you made it. Come on in."

"You gave me good directions, although, with all the planted fields, I was starting to think I'd missed a turn or taken a wrong one somewhere." She followed him up the steps, then walked through the doorway into a light-infused foyer. The floor appeared to be the original hardwood, and the light oak made the space feel warm and inviting. The pale-yellow walls with white trim looked fresh and created an ambiance that felt both cheerful and welcoming.

"I love it, Levi. The paint colors and the wood are just so ... amiable and calming."

He grinned at her. "Glad you think so. That was what I was going for. These days, I need all the peacefulness I can find."

She started to shift into her nursing mentality. To ask him questions about his health, both physical and mental, but that wasn't why she was here. Besides, she knew it would bother him for her to ask even one clarifying question.

Proof of that existed in how he'd reacted to her the day they'd met. For his sake, she'd make sure another nurse on staff was assigned to him for his next appointment. The last thing she wanted was for Levi to feel uncomfortable at the hospital in her presence because they'd started dating. It was a simple thing to surmise his male ego or pride might feel bruised if she was there when he likely felt quite vulnerable. Men were funny creatures that way, at least they were if Levi was anything like her father and brothers.

He led her through the dining room into the kitchen, where she set the container of cookies on the counter and glanced around at the white cabinets, the walls with the lightest tint of green, and the magnificent views outside through the large windows. She could see a pasture in the distance with horses grazing beside a small barn that was painted yellow instead of the traditional red.

"It's lovely here, Levi. I can see why you wanted to remodel this place and live here."

"Thanks. I have several more projects to finish, like furniture shopping, but it's getting there. I'm afraid it's going to rain at some point this afternoon. Do you want to go try out the pistol before it does?"

"Sure." Grace opened the gun case Levi had placed on the counter and extracted the pink-handled pistol.

He whistled softly as she held it out to him and gave it a thorough inspection as he held it in his hand. "Nickel-plated, double-action, five-shot revolver. Boy, is it light. I bet it doesn't even weigh a pound." He moved his hand up and down, as though guessing the weight of the pistol as he held it. "Looks to be a .32 caliber. I've got plenty of ammo, and I've already set up some targets."

"Then let's go see how it shoots." Grace closed the lid of the case and set her purse on the floor at the end of the counter.

Levi handed the pistol to her and led the way out the kitchen door and around the side of the house to a carport. He opened the door of an old blue pickup that had a double gun rack across the back window.

Grace glanced at the shotgun and rifle that were in the rack and a small wooden crate holding boxes of ammunition on the seat as she slid in. From the hay leaves on the floor to the shovel and pitchfork in the bed, the pickup was obviously used for work on the farm.

"Is this your work pickup?" she asked when Levi got in and backed out of the carport. It had room for three vehicles, although the only other one in it was his orange pickup.

"It is. What gave it away? The dirt and hay leaves? Or the smell of fertilizer I can't get rid of no matter how long I leave the windows rolled down?"

Grace laughed. "The shovel in the back." She looked into the bed again. "Are those gopher traps?"

Levi nodded. "Yes. They are a never-ending problem. Them and ground squirrels. Pop and I are about ready for our annual shooting competition, so it's good I'll get in some practice with you today."

She wrinkled her forehead in confusion. "Shooting competition?"

Levi grinned at her as they drove away from the house on a dirt lane that wound past a pond where a few dozen head of Hereford cattle grazed in almost belly-deep grass. "Around the first of June, we are typically overrun with ground squirrels. They cause more damage than you can imagine, especially on a farm that raises root vegetables. We pick a day, go out, and see how many we can shoot. The winner gets bragging rights, and Ma generally makes the winner's favorite meal for dinner the next day."

"I had no idea the ground squirrels could get so bad here, but I understand how they'd be a nuisance on a row crop farm." Grace gazed around with interest, fascinated with the well-tended fields they passed. Levi turned onto what appeared to be a path and parked the pickup a dozen yards away from a stack of straw bales. Several targets of varying sizes were propped in front of the bales on stands made from what appeared to be old pieces of plywood and two-by-fours.

"The straw is used for bedding, so don't worry if the bullets go astray into a bale. It won't hurt anything."

"Good to know," Grace said as she hurried out of the pickup before Levi could come around to open her door. She was too excited to test out the pink pistol to wait for social niceties.

Levi lifted the crate of ammunition and carried it to the tailgate of the pickup that he'd already opened. She couldn't help but watch the muscles in his arm bunch beneath the cotton of the blue plaid western shirt he wore that made his eyes even bluer. His jeans were worn and faded, and the brown cowboy boots on his feet were dusty with scuffed toes, but the casual, comfortable way he wore his clothes assured her he wasn't pretending to be a country boy but lived the life of one.

His right hand was bare, but he'd pulled a leather glove over his left one. It looked like he'd stuffed the empty fingers. She wished she could tell him to take it off, that his hand didn't bother her, but she was afraid of offending him. Until Levi came to terms with his injury and stopped letting it rule his opinion of himself, there wasn't anything she could do to help him.

Nevertheless, she found herself increasingly attracted to the good-looking farmer with a boyish smile and a tender heart.

"Here's what you need for that little pistol," he said, lifting a small box from the crate. "You know how to load it?"

Grace shrugged. She'd been shooting guns with her brothers since she was eight, but something held her back from informing Levi of the fact. He took a few bullets from the box, talked her through inserting the rounds into the chamber and closing it, then walked with her over to the targets.

He offered simple instructions for shooting the pistol.

She feigned a look of confusion and bit back a satisfied smile when Levi moved behind her, wrapped his arms around her, and lightly placed his hand over hers. Her intention had been to get him to help her, and her devious plan had worked even better than she'd hoped.

The scent of him—of sunshine and outdoors mingling with a hint of leather—intrigued her senses while his warmth enveloped her within its embrace. Electrical currents zinged through her from his touch as her limbs grew languid.

She could have stayed right there all day, in the circle of his arms, but he might eventually notice her hesitancy to attempt shooting the target and question why.

Grace adjusted her grip on the pink pistol slightly, closed one eye, sighted the target, and pulled off a shot that hit the center of a bullseye.

"Lucky shot," Levi whispered in her ear. The heat of his breath on her neck made a delicious shiver slide along her spine while her heart hammered in her chest. "You've been holding out on me, you little stinker."

Slowly, she turned her head toward his and waited for the impact of his lips on hers, only he didn't kiss her. As the fog of yearning lifted, she realized he'd taken a step back and was giving her a look she couldn't quite read.

"You've done this before, haven't you?" he asked, as a grin spread across his kissable lips.

"Only a few hundred times," Grace admitted. "My dad takes it as a personal insult if I let my brothers beat me when we're shooting targets. He taught me everything he knows about guns and shooting."

Levi rolled his eyes and stepped back. "I should have known the farm girl would know how to shoot."

Grace shrugged again, finished shooting the rounds still in the chamber, hitting a bullseye every time, then walked back to the pickup and loaded the pistol again.

"It's a really nice gun, Levi. Give it a try," she said, handing it to him. She could tell he wanted to shoot it, and since it was so lightweight, she knew he could easily handle it one-handed.

"You don't have to tell me twice. This piece was made by a fine craftsman. And you say it once belonged to Annie Oakley?" he asked as they walked closer to the targets.

"There's a piece of parchment in the case, yellowed with age, that gives proof to that claim. As far as Adelaide Brennan owning it …" she paused for dramatic effect, lifting her shoulders in a shrug, "that is anyone's guess."

"Didn't she star in …" They discussed old movies for a moment, then Levi took aim and fired the pistol, hitting the bullseye of the target on all five shots.

"This really is a great weapon, Grace. Thank you for letting me shoot it."

"Of course. Want to try it again?"

He nodded and went to reload it. "But only after you give it another try."

Although she loved the little pink pistol, Grace had the most fun when Levi handed her the shotgun and let her shoot the clay pigeons he lobbed into the air using a hand thrower.

"If I were just guessing, I'd say you are enthralled by shooting clay pigeons. I think you only missed one." Levi smiled at her, and she could see his pride for her on his face as well as hear it in his voice.

"I wouldn't have missed that one, but I got distracted." She wouldn't tell him he was the reason for the distraction. She'd been so intently watching Levi as he tossed the clay pigeon that she hadn't gathered her wits in time to shoot.

"Can Cindy shoot as well as you?" Levi asked as they walked back to the pickup.

Grace couldn't contain the unladylike snort that rolled out of her. Levi gave her a look of surprise, then grinned broadly.

"I'll take that as no," he said as he set the shotgun in the gun rack in the pickup after checking a second time to make sure it wasn't loaded.

"Cindy is not into guns, vehicles, or most sports. She does enjoy going for walks and spending time outdoors when the weather is nice, but she's not one who would ever jump into a game of baseball or eagerly work up a sweat running."

"Are you? Eager to run, I mean?"

Grace shook her head. "Not particularly, but I do enjoy a good baseball game from time to time."

It was on the tip of her tongue to ask what sports he liked, but then she thought of his hand and the new limitations he imposed upon himself and thought better of it.

"Would you like a tour of my house before we head over to Ma and Pop's place for dinner?"

"I'd love that," Grace said, allowing Levi to open the pickup door for her. When he slid behind the wheel, she looked over at him. "Are you sure I won't be imposing?"

"Not at all. Ma is beside herself with excitement that you're coming, and Pop promised not to ask too many questions." Levi put the truck in gear, and they headed back to his place.

He introduced her to his horses, and Grace happily greeted a freckled, homely mutt when it ran over to them. "That's Spreckles. She's a good dog and friend."

"What breed is she?" Grace asked as she knelt down and gave the dog several scratches behind her ears and rubs along her back.

"I have no idea. She looks like someone dumped a dozen different breeds in a blender and that's what poured out when they were all mixed together."

Grace laughed, gave the dog one more pat, then stood. "She does have interesting coloring."

"Interesting," Levi said with a grin. "You mean odd and strange. I think she's got every color ever painted on a dog, then the freckles thrown in for good measure to make sure not a single one was missed."

"Still, she seems like a sweet girl." Grace smiled at the dog trailing behind them as Levi showed her the barn, which was mostly used for storage and had a nice tack room near the door. Maybe her farmer was more cowboy than she gave him credit for being. That thought was affirmed when he invited her to come out riding whenever she liked.

Inside the house, he showed her the living room, which she'd only gotten a peek at earlier, then walked with her down the hall, pointing out the bathroom. They stepped into a spacious family room with built-in bookcases surrounding a big rock fireplace. Grace thought it was wonderful, with the windows offering a view of the backyard that stretched into fields in the distance.

However, furniture was sparse throughout the house. The living room had one end table with a lamp attached to it and a well-worn chair from the 1940s. The family room had a couch that looked like a relic from the previous century with an upturned wooden apple box for an end table.

"You really do need to go furniture shopping," she said, looking around the near-empty room.

"I know. Any thoughts on what you'd get?" Levi asked.

Grace hesitated to share her opinions, but he seemed genuinely interested in hearing them. "This is such a nice, big room. You need a long couch, leather, probably dark brown, to anchor it. I'd get a couple of side chairs, maybe even something like a

Berkline recliner. I'd stick with solid wood in a simple design for end tables and coffee table, and go for lamps that are neutral. If you want to have a western theme, you could do that with throw pillows and the art on the walls, and maybe even get a Pendleton wool blanket to throw on the end of the couch for extra color. Or whatever you wanted."

Levi stared at her for a moment, then grabbed her hand and hustled back to the living room. "What about in here?"

Grace studied the beautiful pale-yellow walls with the contrasting white trim and envisioned how she'd decorate it if money were not a concern. "I'd go very classy and traditional in here. Timeless pieces that defy trends. You could put a grouping of chairs around this lovely marble fireplace, then have a few more over here by the window with the couch facing out. Over in the corner by the built-in bookcase, would be perfect for a desk and leather chair." She moved to the opposite corner of the room. "A grandfather clock or a curio cabinet might look nice here."

Levi had followed her around the room, as though he was picturing in his mind the furniture she described. He asked her about color and fabric choices, and then they returned to the kitchen where she offered him the cookies she'd made.

He tasted one and gave her a surprised look as he snagged two more. "These are delicious—so soft and flavorful. I've never had pineapple cookies, but they're really good. Thanks for bringing them."

"You're welcome." She took one, then snapped the lid on before she glanced at her watch. Levi had mentioned heading over to have dinner with his parents at five. They would need to leave soon. "If I promise not to spill crumbs on the floor, may I see the rest of the house."

"Spill crumbs all you like. Spreckles is like a vacuum when I let her in." They passed through the dining room with a built-in china cabinet, then started up the stairs located in the foyer. "I've got two of the four bedrooms set up. You can tell me what you think."

Grace thought the upstairs was wonderful with amazing views out the bedroom windows and two bathrooms for the four bedrooms to share. The furniture in the two bedrooms Levi had set up looked old and expensive but fit the house well. She could imagine curling up on the window seat in the south-facing bedroom and watching the clouds roll in for hours or getting lost in a good book.

"I love the rooms and the furniture, Levi. Are the pieces family heirlooms?"

"I assume so. I found them in the attic. There's a lot more stuff up there. I just need to sort through it and figure out what is usable and what I'll have to buy. I think I can find most of what I'll need for the living room up there." He motioned for her to precede him downstairs. "I really appreciate the ideas you shared, Grace. It's a big help. Ma keeps giving me samples and magazine ads for modern styles and colors I don't like, but I know she's only trying to be helpful."

"I'm happy to share my limited insight. I think what you've done so far is fabulous, Levi. Your home has a very peaceful, relaxing vibe, even without furniture filling the rooms."

Her comments appeared to please him, judging by his smile as he walked with her to the kitchen. He helped her clean the pistol before stowing it back in the case, and then she carried it and her purse out to her car. Levi held open his pickup door for her, and they drove to his parents' home on the other end of the farm. Nerves made her stomach clench the entire drive there.

What if his mother hated her? What if his dad didn't like her? What if she made a complete idiot of herself over dinner? What if someone realized how much she was coming to care for Levi even though she'd only known him a few weeks?

The thought of how much she did care for him, how often he was in her thoughts and prayers, brought her up short. Although she would deny it if anyone brought it up, she was really starting to fall for Levi.

How was that possible?

She'd had boyfriends she'd dated for months. One she'd even dated for more than a year. Not one of them had made her feel such powerful emotions as Levi did. When she was around him, she felt excited and nervous, and energized all at once. When they were apart, she felt lonesome in a way she'd never experienced before meeting him.

What was she doing? Thinking? She was so busy with work she barely had time to keep her uniform clean. Would she really have time to invest in a relationship? And what if that wasn't what Levi had in mind? What if he only wanted to be friends?

What if he was one of the guys who got a crush on his nurse? Maybe that was all shooting targets and eating pie and going to the movies was about.

Then she dared to glance across the pickup cab, and her gaze tangled with Levi's. What she saw in the marvelous blue depths of his eyes made her catch her breath.

Maybe she was trying to convince herself what was happening between them—the magnetic pull— was only in her imagination so she wouldn't have to deal with the reality that she was falling in love with Levi Gibson.

Rattled by that revelation, she followed him into his parents' home in a daze, trying to compartmentalize her feelings while summoning her best manners.

It wasn't until Levi shut the door behind them that she even recalled she wore a hat. She whipped it off and did her best to fluff her hair with her fingers while Levi hung her hat on a coat rack just inside the door.

He walked with her past a living room full of wagon wheel furniture that drew out her smile and a formal dining room with foil wallpaper patterned with flocked flowers, then led her down a hallway to a kitchen filled with pink appliances that made the room appear like something from a dollhouse.

"Hey, Ma," Levi said as they entered the room. "Something sure smells good."

The petite woman standing at the stove turned around, and Grace could immediately see the resemblance between mother and son. Levi had his mother's blonde hair and blue eyes, as well as her smile.

Before he had a chance to offer an introduction, his mother wiped her hands on her pink floral and gingham apron and rushed over to them. She wrapped Grace in a tight hug, then took a step back, capturing Grace's hands in hers. When she offered a friendly smile, her eyes twinkled with something that Grace could only describe as joy.

"I'm so, so happy to meet you, Grace. Is it okay if I call you Grace? What a beautiful name. So well suited to you. You look so graceful and lovely." She glanced at Levi. "She's absolutely stunning, son." Then she turned back to Grace. "Oh, I'm just thrilled you're here."

"Thank you, Mrs. Gibson. I appreciate the invitation to join you for dinner," Grace said, no longer feeling nervous but welcomed. "May I help with anything?"

"Of course, you may." She released Grace's hands, and her smile widened. "But first, let's go sit in the living room and enjoy a few appetizers. Dinner needs to simmer a bit."

Grace watched as Levi's mother bustled over to the refrigerator and extracted a tray full of food. She handed it to Levi, then lifted another that that held a milk glass pitcher with a grapevine pattern and four matching glasses. She thrust it into Grace's hands and then retrieved a third tray from the counter stacked with small plates, napkins, and forks.

"Your father came in a few minutes before you arrived, Levi. He'll join us in a minute," Stella said as she led the way to the living room.

Grace ended up sitting next to Levi on the leather couch stitched with saddles along the back cushions while Stella took a seat in the chair closest to her.

"Levi mentioned you work at the VA Hospital. That must be so hard to see all the sick and wounded come through your doors."

Grace accepted the glass of lemonade the woman held out to her and took a sip, needing a moment to formulate her reply. "It's hard to see them in pain and suffering, but I pray my work there can ease that a little while offering hope and help."

Levi's mother gave her a long, intense look, then handed Grace a little plate that held two tiny cheese balls rolled in crushed pecans, and a deviled egg, as well as two carrot curls skewered with a toothpick and topped with a black olive.

A man who looked like an older version of Levi, albeit with brown hair and gray eyes, hurried into the room. From the moisture still clinging to his hair, Grace assumed he'd just taken a shower. He walked straight over to Grace with his hand extended in welcome. When she stood to shake it, he sandwiched her hand between both of his. She could feel the calluses on his palms and fingers and knew Levi's father worked hard on the farm. His hands reminded her so much of her father's, and it made a wave of homesickness wash over her.

"Gary Gibson," the man said, smiling kindly. "It's sure nice to meet you, Miss Marshall. Welcome to our home."

"It's lovely to be here, sir. Thank you."

He grinned at her, gave Levi a playful swat on his leg, then took the glass and plate Stella held out to him before settling into the chair nearest the other end of the couch.

"You have three brothers?" Stella asked, and the discussion changed to family and Grace's years growing up in Holiday.

Gary asked about her family's dairy and the types of crops grown in the area. He mentioned meeting a few members of the Coleman family, one of the oldest and most prominent in Holiday, at a bull sale a few years ago.

"Come on, Grace. You can help me finish up the meal," Stella said, rising to her feet when Grace had finished the last bite of the delicious cheese ball on her plate. The deviled egg had been different than any she'd ever tasted, but it was good too.

She refused to let her panic show, though, as she lifted the appetizer tray and followed the powerhouse that was Levi's mother to the kitchen. She might be small in stature, but she had a huge, irrepressible personality. One that currently intimidated Grace.

Then again, it might have been far harder if Levi's mother were quiet and timid and left Grace wondering if she liked or detested her. With Stella, every thought and emotion passed across her face as though she were a wide-open book waiting to be read.

The woman was nothing like Grace had expected, but she found herself drawn to Stella's openness and lively manner.

"How may I help?" Grace asked as she set the tray on the counter near the sink, then pushed up the sleeves of her sweater.

Stella quickly set what was left of the appetizers in the refrigerator, then motioned to a drawer near the stove. "The potato masher is in there, and there's butter and salt in that cupboard right by your head, darling. If you wouldn't mind mashing the potatoes, that would be most helpful."

"Sure." Grace washed her hands, drained the potatoes, and set about mashing them, adding a generous amount of butter and seasoning them with salt until they were smooth and creamy. She set the lid back over the pot to keep them warm, then looked over to see Stella buttering the tops on a pan of hot rolls. The yeasty smell filled the kitchen with a mouth-watering aroma that blended with the aroma of rich spices emanating from the oven.

"I hope you don't mind eating in here, Grace. The dining room is nice but not very cozy for just the four of us," Stella said, offering an apologetic look. "I also know my husband and son well, and they have never managed to eat Swiss steak without slopping it on the tablecloth, the floor, or themselves."

Grace laughed. "Is that what smells so good?"

Stella beamed as she set the rolls into a cloth-lined basket. "I'm glad you think it does. Honestly, those men of mine are just a step above cavedwellers, but I've tried to train them."

Grace grinned and took the basket from Stella, setting it on a lovely round antique oak table that was positioned in front of a large bay window. The view from the window looked out over the backyard which seemed enormous. A short wooden fence divided it from the edge of a potato field.

When she turned her attention from outdoors to the table, white Noritake china adorned with pink roses and gray leaves in the center of each plate gleamed in the waning light. A beautiful crystal bowl of pink peonies rested in the center of the table.

"Your dish pattern is beautiful, Mrs. Gibson." Grace turned around and picked up the salad bowl Stella had set on the counter, carrying it to the table.

"Thank you. It was a wedding gift from my mother-in-law. She knew how much I loved pink." Stella gave her a long glance. "What's your favorite color?"

"Teal blue." Grace shrugged. "I don't know why for certain, other than it reminds me of being outside with my dad and brothers at the lake near our home. My mother was so disappointed I was a tomboy for most of my childhood. She had visions of pink dresses dripping in lace, ballet lessons, and afternoon tea parties. Only, I preferred wearing overalls, detested dance lessons, and was more apt to make a mud pie to throw at my brothers than quietly sip tea."

Stella laughed. "You sound like my kind of girl, Grace. I liked to play outside with my brothers when I was young. My older sister filled my mother's need for someone to walk in her footsteps." She pulled a big, heavy pan from the oven and hustled over to the table, setting it on a long cast iron trivet. "Whew. I should have left that for Gary, but I think we're ready to eat. If you'll summon the men, I'll get the drinks."

Grace retraced her steps to the living room where Levi and his father discussed irrigation practices. They both stood when she entered the room. "Mrs. Marshall said the food is ready."

"I'm starving," Gary said, quickly setting empty appetizer plates and glasses on the tray that had held the drinks. "Good thing I was out working where I couldn't smell that steak cooking all afternoon, or I wouldn't have been worth a plug nickel."

He lifted the tray and left the room. Levi picked up the other tray and glanced at the coffee table to make sure nothing had been left behind, then offered Grace a questioning look.

"You doing okay? Mom didn't give you a stiff interrogation, did she?"

Grace started to reach for the tray, then tucked her hands into the front pockets of her jeans. Levi wouldn't appreciate her offer of help.

She shook her head and lowered her voice to a whisper. "No interrogation. She's a lot of fun, Levi. From the way you talked about her, I envisioned a dragon in a ruffled apron."

A bark of laughter escaped from him. "Just wait until one of us riles her. You'll get to witness the transformation from fun-loving housewife to angry dragon lady."

Grace shook her head. "I doubt that very much. I might have to ask her for the cheese ball recipe. Cindy would go nuts for them."

He grinned. "Pun intended?"

Grace winked at him as they walked down the hallway and into the kitchen. Gary pulled out Stella's chair at the table, and she took a seat. Levi slid the tray onto the counter, then pulled out the chair next to his mother. Grace sank into it with a nod to Levi.

Levi took a seat next to her, then slid his hand beneath the table to clasp hers. She watched him from the corner of her eye as he bowed his head.

Grace followed suit and listened as Gary offered thanks for the meal and included a few words about Grace that made her glad she'd overcome her fear of meeting Levi's parents and joined them that evening.

As they ate, Levi's parents asked her questions and also answered hers about their farm, the types of potatoes they favored, and the process of extracting sugar from the beets they grew. She'd had no idea there were so many different types of potatoes or that new varieties were being developed all the time. It made sense that improvements in pest and disease-resistant potatoes would be a huge benefit to their operation.

"We're too stuffed for dessert now, Ma. How about we wait a little while?" Levi asked as he helped clear the table.

The meal had been so tasty Grace had even allowed herself to have a second helping of the tender Swiss steak and an extra scoop of what Stella had called overnight salad. The dinner rolls had been soft and warm and incredibly good when topped with butter and a dollop of homemade strawberry jam.

"That's fine, honey. Why don't you and Grace take a walk before the rain starts?" Stella motioned toward the window with her elbow as she lifted a bowl in each hand.

"I should help with the dishes," Grace said, carrying dishes to the sink.

"Nonsense. It won't make Gary break out in hives to help." Stella tossed a sassy look at her husband.

He feigned indignation but smacked a kiss on Stella's cheek as he lifted a stack of plates and carried them to the sink.

"Come on before she changes her mind," Levi whispered in Grace's ear, taking her hand in his and leading her to the front of the house. Grace snagged Cindy's hat and plopped it on her head as they rushed outside and down the front walk.

Levi headed in the opposite direction from which they'd driven to the house. They meandered past a big red barn, equipment sheds, and a shop with tall doors propped open. Inside, a tractor appeared to be in the midst of a repair with parts scattered around it on the cement floor.

"I should probably close these in case it does rain," Levi said, veering over to the shop. It only took him a moment to pull up an iron rod that fit into a hole in the cement pad outside the shop and push one door closed, then repeat the process on the other. He disappeared inside for a moment, then returned, brushing his good hand on the leg of his jeans. "Sorry about that. If the wind catches the doors, they can flap back and forth like a sail in a storm, and it damages the frame."

"No problem." Grace liked the feel of Levi's warm hand enveloping hers when he took her hand in his again, and they continued meandering down the road. The gravel crunching beneath their feet was the only sound in the stillness other than the noise of a few birds chirping in the distance.

The buildings were behind them and a curve in the road was ahead of them when they stopped to stare at the sky. It had turned from a grayish hue to shades of azure and tangerine when the sun popped out from behind the clouds as it made its evening descent toward the horizon.

Grace drew in a deep breath of the fresh air, savoring the scents of just-cut alfalfa and a Russian olive tree in bloom. The scents and sounds of being in the country were some of the things she missed most while living in the city.

It wasn't often she and Cindy made time to watch the sunset, not that they had a good view of it from their apartment anyway.

Grace intended to savor every moment of this opportunity. She placed her hand on top of the hat she wore, tipped her head back, and closed her eyes, and one at a time, let her senses fill.

When she opened her eyes, the sky was a dazzling display that imbued her with bliss. She looked back over her shoulder to see Levi intently watching her instead of the sunset.

Grace smiled and stretched her hand out to him. He stepped forward, not taking the hand she offered, but moving behind her, wrapping his right hand around her waist, then settling his left hand over the top of it, encircling her with his presence.

She took another deep breath, tantalized by his masculine scent as it blended with the fresh breeze that wafted with a hint of the coming rainstorm.

Grace lost all track of time, all sense of place or purpose. All she knew at that moment was how good, how amazingly right it felt to be there with Levi. To stand in the circle of his arms and rest against his solid chest, and let the splendor of God's creation fill her heart until it felt like it might burst with love.

A cold, chilly drop of liquid fell on her hands as she rested them on top of Levi's at the center of her waist. She glanced up and caught a big drop of rain in her eye and two on her cheek.

"Come on. We'd better run for it, or you'll be soaked." Levi shouted to be heard over the thunder that rumbled right before lightning cracked across the sky. He grabbed Grace's hand in his and sprinted toward the house. He pulled her under the eave of the porch as the clouds burst and rain poured down in sheets.

Grace leaned against him, entranced by the heat that suddenly sizzled in his blue eyes. What might have happened next was unexpectedly interrupted when Stella opened the door and tugged Grace inside.

"Good lands, son! She might freeze to death out there in this chilly storm." Stella frowned at Levi as he stepped into the entry and closed the door behind him. He lifted Grace's hat from her head and set it on the coat rack.

Grace heard Gary mutter, "The boy likely had a few ideas for keeping her warm before you butted in, Stell," and had a hard time holding back her laughter, especially when she looked at Levi, and he waggled his eyebrows at her.

Somehow Gary's comment made her feel like part of the family. The conversation flowed with the ease of good friends as they enjoyed lemon bars with homemade lemon ice cream and cups of coffee in the living room.

At the end of the evening, Stella invited Grace to spend the night so she wouldn't have to drive home in the rain, but she politely refused. After thanking his parents for a lovely evening, Levi drove her back to his place to get her car.

"Are you sure I can't drive you home?" he asked, stopping his pickup close to her car so she could basically go from one door to the other without getting too wet in the process.

"I'm sure, Levi. I've driven in the rain plenty of times. I had such a nice time with you today. Thank you for letting me come out and shoot the pistol as well as see the farm."

"I'm the one who should thank you for hanging out with me and enduring dinner with my parents."

"Your mom and dad are fantastic. They both have a great sense of humor, and they really made me feel welcome. Besides, your mother is an amazing cook. How do you stay in such great shape with all the good food she makes?"

"Work. Just the day-to-day work of a farmer."

Grace knew that type of work well from growing up on her family's dairy farm. "Thanks again for inviting me to come today." She scooted closer on the bench seat and gave him a hug as the gear shift pressed into her thigh. She'd anticipated lingering a few minutes, savoring their first real kiss, but Levi merely gave her a hug in return, then kissed her cheek. Granted, he seemed concerned about the growing darkness and increasing severity of the storm and her driving home in it. But still, she'd been looking forward to finding out if he was as good at kissing as she imagined him to be.

"Call you tomorrow?" he asked, his hand on the door handle.

"Definitely. Thanks again, Levi." She watched as he jumped out and raced around the pickup, head ducked against the pelting rain.

He opened her car door then the pickup door, and moved back.

Grace tossed Cindy's hat into the car so it wouldn't get wet, then got out of the pickup and looked at Levi one last time before leaving. His hair was plastered to his head from the rain, and his shirt was soaked to the skin, outlining defined muscles in his shoulders and arms. The heat was back in his eyes, burning like an incandescent flame.

A flame that might consume her if she let it.

Before she did something she shouldn't, she turned to get into her car but suddenly found herself hauled against Levi's hard chest. His arms encircled her again, and she felt the weight of his hands at the back of her waist.

She leaned into him, into his strength, and let her fingers twine into the damp tendrils of his hair at the back of his head.

His gaze fused to hers, as though he searched for something and found what he needed before his lips touched hers gently, tenderly.

A soft groan escaped from Grace, and Levi pulled her closer. He deepened the kiss—exploring, demanding, giving.

Grace felt lost in that moment.

Lost to the emotion swirling through her. Lost to anything but how perfect it was to be with Levi, to give herself over to the rapture of receiving and returning his powerful kisses.

When he finally raised his head, water dripped into their eyes and ran down their chins, but she smiled, and he kissed her again.

"You need to go," he shouted to be heard above the storm.

"I know!" Instead of leaving, she pulled his head back down for one more intense kiss that left her senses so addled she wasn't sure she could remember her own name, let alone how to drive home.

"I could do this all night, Grace, but I can't let you stay." Without warning, Levi lifted her up and set her in the car, kissed her cheek, and then closed her door.

He mouthed "good night" and stood in the rain, watching her leave. Even in her rearview mirror as she looked back, he remained rooted in place, observing her departure.

Chilled from the rain and the unfamiliar sensations coursing through her, Grace turned the heat on high and drove home.

A smile slowly spread across her face. Levi Gibson was an even better kisser than she'd imagined.

"Grab me one of those breakfast bars, please, then let's hustle," Grace called to Cindy as she shoved her feet into a pair of red slingback sandals and laced up the ties on the front.

"Got them. Would Levi eat one?" Cindy asked, leaning around the doorway in the kitchen.

"Probably, even though I'm sure he ate something wonderful like eggs and bacon and fresh berry muffins baked by his mother for breakfast."

Cindy laughed and reappeared with three chocolate chip breakfast bars. "How on earth did you talk Levi into taking us shopping today? Don't men hate that sort of thing?"

"Generally, yes, but I think he's just glad for whatever time we get to spend together." Grace glanced down at the navy peasant blouse she'd tucked into a navy skirt with wide red and narrow white stripes running horizontally across it. With four big navy buttons for trim, two on each side of the high waist, she hoped the outfit looked cute.

Cindy, who could usually sense her thoughts, gave her an approving nod. "You look amazing. It appears your hair is being more cooperative than usual today."

Grace grinned and glanced in the mirror. This morning she'd used a little extra styling product to get it to hang straight, parted down the middle. How long the style would last was anyone's guess.

Most of the time, her thick, wavy hair had a mind of its own. As long as she could get it contained in a bun for work, the rest of the time she didn't worry about it too much. But since she'd started dating Levi, vanity won over convenience, and she'd spent more time than she cared to admit trying to tame her hair.

"Just hope the rain stays away, or I'll have a frizzy, wavy mess in my face all day."

"Rain, rain, go away …" Cindy chanted.

A knock at the door caused Grace to give Cindy a look full of anticipation. She turned the knob and pulled open the door to find Levi standing there, straw cowboy hat in his left hand, wearing a cotton plaid western shirt in hues of light tan and bright blue, accentuating the blue of his eyes and the breadth of his shoulders.

"Howdy, ma'am," he greeted in a drawl that caused both Grace and Cindy to laugh.

"Did you take a trip to Texas you failed to mention when I spoke to you Thursday?" Grace asked as she grabbed a white sweater and her purse, then waited for Cindy to step out to close the apartment door behind them.

"Nope, but I thought I'd see if I could pull it off. How did I do?" he asked as they hurried downstairs.

"Tolerably well, cowboy." Cindy nodded her thanks to him when he held open the door as they left the lobby. "Are you sure you want to take the two of us shopping?"

"I'm here, aren't I?" Levi grinned at them both, then opened his pickup door when they reached it.

Grace took his hand and got in, sliding into the middle, and Cindy jumped in beside her.

Once they were on their way to Nampa, Cindy broke out the breakfast bars. Grace unwrapped one and handed it to Levi.

"What's this?" he asked, then took a big bite.

"A breakfast bar. They're supposed to be full of nutrients." Grace bit off a small piece, then grinned at Levi. "We mostly eat them because they are chocolate chip bars dipped in chocolate, but they have the word breakfast on the box, so we don't feel guilty about indulging in them first thing in the morning."

"Candy for breakfast," he muttered, then hurriedly ate the rest of the bar in two bites.

Levi rolled down the window and the fresh air blew into the pickup cab. It felt so good, Grace wouldn't even complain about what it was doing to her carefully styled hair.

"Do you two often spend your Saturdays shopping?" Levi questioned, glancing first at Cindy, then at Grace.

"Not often, but my cousin's wedding is next weekend, and we need new outfits to wear." Grace gave Levi a long glance. They'd been dating for six weeks now, but she still tried to convince herself it was just a passing thing. However, the strong current of connection she experienced every time they were together was unlike anything she'd ever known or even dreamed of experiencing. Being with Levi was easy and enjoyable. She felt like she'd known him forever, even as she kept peeling back one layer after another to find more things about him that she loved.

Although she hadn't said the words to him yet, nor had he verbalized them to her, Grace was sure he cared for her as deeply as she was coming to care for him.

Regardless, they both held themselves back. For what reason, she wasn't sure. After watching Cindy lose her fiancé and seeing the wounded men who came to the hospital, Grace should have run headlong into love, knowing how short and precious life could be. Something, though, made her hesitate with Levi. The part of her that liked to analyze things thought it was perhaps because he still needed time to heal and come to terms with his injuries and the scars, both mental and physical, that he would always carry.

Grace released a long breath. It was such a lovely day, far too lovely for such deep thoughts.

She intended just to enjoy the time spent with Levi and Cindy.

Levi had promised to treat them to lunch at Karcher Mall after they finished shopping. Not only was it the biggest mall in the whole valley, but it was also the first mall constructed in the state of Idaho. Grace and Cindy hadn't gone there often, but when they did, they generally made a day of it, visiting all the stores and eating at the restaurant located midway in the mall.

Today promised to be amusing, enlightening, and entertaining with Levi along. He claimed his mother had asked him to pick up a gift for a baby shower while he was there. Grace knew that meant she and Cindy would get to choose it, and she looked forward to perusing the baby items in the department stores.

For now, though, she relished being pressed close to Levi as they drove to Nampa. She adjusted the dial on the radio until she found a station playing popular music of the day. Levi preferred country music, but Grace enjoyed a variety of musical styles.

Cindy grinned at her, and they both started singing along as Sammy Davis Jr. crooned about the candy man. Levi rolled his eyes with great exaggeration, but when they got to the chorus, she heard him humming the tune.

After the song ended, they listened to a news report.

"Sources have confirmed Elvis and Priscilla Presley have separated and filed for divorce. In honor of the King, here is one of my favorite songs," the disc jockey said.

All three of them remained silent as Elvis sang, "Can't Help Falling in Love with You."

"That's so sad," Cindy said when the song ended. Grace turned down the volume of the radio.

"It's tragic. And they have that sweet little girl. I wonder what will happen to her." Grace hated to think of anyone splitting up, especially when a child was involved.

"Hey, did you hear about Billie Jean King winning the French Open?" Levi asked in an obvious effort to change the subject.

"No. That's exciting. I can't imagine ever playing tennis as well as she does," Cindy said, leaning around Grace. "I loved tennis in high school, but golly, that girl can sure dazzle on the court."

From there, they shifted to lighter topics, and before they knew it, they'd arrived at the mall.

Levi pulled into a parking space, and the three of them ventured inside the red-carpeted shopping center that seemed both opulent and fun.

They stopped for a moment to study a taxidermy display of a huge polar bear with a seal inside a big glass-enclosed case.

"I'm sure glad I wasn't the one who encountered him while he was alive," Levi said, then lunged at Grace with his good hand extended like a claw, making deep, growling noises. She darted behind Cindy, the three of them laughing as they walked away from the case and made their way to a large department store.

While Grace and Cindy tried on numerous dresses, Levi disappeared, but he returned as they were asking a salesgirl to hold two outfits for them.

"Aren't you buying the dresses you picked out?" Levi asked in confusion as Cindy led the way out of the store.

"Not yet. We want to see if we find something we like better. If we don't, we'll come back and get those. If she doesn't hold them for us and we decide we want them, someone else might come in and buy them," Grace explained.

A look of confusion settled over his face as they wandered down the mall concourse to a dress shop.

"I'll meet you back here in half an hour," he said, then headed toward the music store.

By the time they were ready for lunch, Cindy and Grace had both found dresses they loved, but at different stores. They intended to go back and get them as soon as they'd eaten, then they'd help Levi select a baby gift.

He escorted them to the mall's restaurant, and they were soon seated on the second level that looked down on the shoppers rushing by below.

She and Cindy enjoyed plates full of chicken salad served on a crisp bed of lettuce and cups of fresh fruit while Levi gobbled up a turkey club sandwich.

He accompanied them to get the dresses she and Cindy had chosen, and as they stopped in the other shops to release the dresses the sales clerks had held for them. When they returned to the main department store, Cindy led the way to the baby department, where Levi looked terrified of catching something contagious.

"Has the baby already arrived?" Grace asked, hoping to shift his focus to the reason why they were there instead of whatever thoughts were racing through his head.

"I have no idea. Ma said it was a cousin, but I think it's a cousin two or three times removed. I barely even recognized the name when she mentioned it. She said to buy something cute and not spend more than ten dollars."

Grace eyed Cindy, and the two of them began sorting through baby blankets and clothes. They were both practically giddy with excitement when they found an outfit that included shorts and socks, a footed sleeper, and a receiving blanket all in the same adorable Winnie-the-Pooh print. The total for the three pieces was less than seven dollars.

Levi gladly handed over the cash.

"Do you want to get it gift-wrapped?" the sales clerk asked, then glanced dismissively at Levi before turning to Cindy and Grace, as though a man couldn't provide the answer.

Levi shook his head and took the bag from the clerk. "My mother will want to examine every thread of these and then wrap it herself, but thank you."

The clerk smiled and wished them a beautiful afternoon before they left the store.

"Anyone hungry?" Levi asked as they walked past the entrance to the grocery store.

"If you are, get whatever you want. We're going to check out that store right over there."

Grace pointed to a high-end boutique where she would never dream of shopping, but it would be neat to look.

Cindy trailed after her as Levi disappeared inside the store.

He held a small paper bag as well as the bag with the baby clothes when he tracked them down in the boutique where they were ogling clothes with price tags that made them afraid to touch anything.

"Ready?" Levi asked, and they left the store together. They plopped onto a couch in one of the seating areas, and then he passed around the Ding Dongs he'd purchased.

The crème filled chocolate cake hit the spot, even if Grace hadn't thought she was hungry. She pulled tissues from her purse to wipe away the sticky residue on their fingers, then waved at one of their neighbors who approached with her two little boys.

"Hello, Mrs. Johnson. Are you enjoying a day of shopping?" Grace asked, greeting the harried-looking woman.

"Not at all, but Tommy and Rick needed new shoes. I swear, their feet grow an inch every other month." The woman held up two shoe boxes tied together with string. "Are you girls having fun?"

"Yes. We have a wedding to attend next weekend and needed new dresses." Grace pointed to the garment bags draped over the couch by Cindy. "Have you met my friend, Mrs. Johnson? This is Levi Gibson."

"Are you the one who drives the orange and white pickup?" the woman asked, grabbing the back belt loop of Tommy's shorts before he could run off.

"Yes, ma'am. It's nice to meet you." Levi stood and tipped his head to her, keeping his cowboy hat covering his hand.

Grace had decided weeks ago he mostly kept the hat with him to hide the wounds on his hand, not because he couldn't go anywhere without it.

"You as well. Unlike some of the hooligans who race through the parking lot, you seem to be a responsible driver."

Grace would have laughed at that, but she didn't want to insult Levi or her neighbor. Levi was a responsible … everything. She couldn't imagine him ever not being dependable, trustworthy, accountable, thoughtful, or honest. It just wasn't in his nature.

"Do you need some help, Mrs. Johnson?" Cindy asked, rising to her feet.

"I was going to pick up a few groceries, then head home, but the boys have reached their limit of good behavior." The woman glared down at her son. The oldest was five and the youngest just three.

"I could watch them for you while you get what you need," Cindy offered. "If you wouldn't mind giving me a ride home."

"We can take you home, Cindy," Grace said, giving her friend a questioning look.

Cindy tipped her head toward Levi and made a shooing motion with her hand.

Apparently, Cindy thought Grace and Levi should spend the rest of the day without a third wheel tagging along. While Grace loved spending time with Levi, she enjoyed being with Cindy as well.

Levi seemed to understand what Cindy was conveying and shook his head. "I'm happy to take you home, Cindy, anytime you want to go."

"Actually, if Mrs. Johnson doesn't object, I could take our things home and then work on the wedding gift I'm making for Delia." Cindy offered their neighbor a hopeful look.

"You'd be doing me a huge favor, Cindy, if you watched the boys. The least I could do in return is give you a ride if you're sure you can stand being cooped up in the car with these two little wild men."

Rick giggled and made a silly face, which his younger brother tried to mimic, only it appeared more like he had a tummy ache, causing them all to laugh.

"Then that's what we'll do." Cindy gave Grace a smug look, then made another shooing motion with her hand.

Grace refused to leave her friend with the two Johnson boys. She'd seen them in action around the apartment building. They were rambunctious on a good day, and she had no doubt that, like their mother had stated, they'd already used up every ounce of their good behavior.

"I'll hurry," Mrs. Johnson said, setting the shoe boxes by their shopping bags and rushing off in the direction of the grocery store where Levi had bought their treats.

Five seconds after she disappeared from sight, the two boys started to whine.

"Should we go look at the polar bear?" Levi asked, hunkering down so he didn't tower over the boys and setting his hat on his head.

"Yes!" they both said excitedly and started to race off, but Levi caught them, holding them like sacks of potatoes against his sides before they got more than a few steps away.

"We'll go look at that big bear," he said, setting them on their feet. "But you boys need to stay with us so you don't get lost. Understand?"

Two little faces nodded up at him.

Levi glanced back at Grace, and she felt her heart melt like chocolate left in the sunshine. Someday, Levi Gibson would make a great dad.

"I'll stay here and keep an eye on our things," Cindy offered, giving Grace a nudge forward.

Grace scowled at her but hurried to reach out a hand to each of the boys.

Levi caught Tommy's other hand with his, and they made their way to the big case that held the polar bear. The boys walked all around it with their eyes wide in wonder. Then they started asking what seemed like dozens of questions about polar bears, if any lived in Boise, and if they would come when it snowed at Christmas.

Their curiosity shifted from polar bears to people they saw walking through the mall, then Tommy pointed to Levi's hand.

"Where are your fingers?" the little one asked in innocence.

Grace tensed, worried Levi would be insulted, reply in anger, or ignore the question.

To her surprise, he knelt down so both boys could look at his hand. He rolled up his shirt sleeve so they could see the wounds that trailed up his arm. He told them he'd been a soldier and some bad men had tried to hurt him and his friends.

"That was mean," Rick said, gingerly touching one of the scars on Levi's forearm. "Does it hurt?"

"Sometimes," Levi answered with honesty.

"Do you miss your fingers?" Tommy asked, holding up his hand and wiggling all his fingers.

"Every day," Levi said, then he held up his hand and pressed his thumb and index finger together like a pincer. "But I'm also grateful every day I still have these two, that I am alive, and can do most things I want to do."

"That's good," Rick said seriously, with his brow furrowed. "I'm sorry you got hurt, Mr. Gibson."

"Thank you, Rick. I appreciate that." Levi rolled down his shirt sleeve and fastened the snaps, stood, and held out both hands to the boys. Tommy latched onto his left index finger while Rick took his right, and they continued back to where Cindy waited.

They'd barely taken a seat on the couch to wait when Mrs. Johnson arrived with her arms full of groceries.

"Let me take those," Levi said, grabbing both big bags from her. Cindy and Grace gathered their things and followed as Mrs. Johnson led the way to her car. She opened the trunk and stowed everything in it, then Cindy gave Grace a hug.

"Have fun with your farmer cowboy. I'll see you later," Cindy whispered in her ear.

Grace smiled at her. "You could come along."

"No. I really do have some things I need to do, and you two need some time together. Between your work and Levi's busy farm schedule, you've hardly seen each other recently. Have a great time."

"I will." Grace backed up and bumped into Levi. He waved at Tommy and Rick as they pressed their noses to the back window of the car after Mrs. Johnson closed the trunk.

"Bye!" Cindy called, and then got in the front seat with Mrs. Johnson and left.

"Well, Miss American Pie, what would you like to do?" Levi asked as Grace wrapped her hand around his right arm, and they headed toward his pickup a few rows over in the parking lot.

She gave him a sly smile. "We could drive the Chevy to the levee, but I heard it was dry."

Levi laughed at her use of a popular song's lyrics. "We could take a drive if you like, just see where the road takes us."

"That sounds great." Grace hopped into the pickup and rolled down the window.

He took her hand in his before he started the pickup and kissed her knuckles, then gave her a long, admiring glance. "I didn't mention it earlier, but you look fantastic today, like a beautiful piece of an American dream come to life."

"Thank you, Levi." She glanced down at her patriotic-hued outfit. "I like these colors."

"I've noticed." He started the pickup and drove out of the parking lot. "You seem to be someone who is proud to be an American."

"Oh, I am," she said, looking at him as he turned down a road bordered by miles of fields, and they drove without a destination in mind. "I might not like the war or the politics involved, or even the politicians, but I love America and what it stands for. I feel it's important to support our country and the people who defend it."

"Me too." Levi shifted into high gear, and they sailed down the road.

With the green fields around them, a blue sky above them, and the afternoon stretching out in front of them, Grace felt so free and happy. She stuck her hand out the window as a new song she liked came on the radio. The Eagles sang about taking it easy, and Grace joined her voice to theirs as her hand bobbed up and down in the breeze like it was riding a wave.

Levi grinned at her. "You are beautiful, Miss Marshall."

"You're not so bad yourself, Mr. Gibson," she said, scooting closer to him. "I know I've mentioned my cousin Delia's wedding about a hundred times, but I don't think I've invited you. If you'd like to come with me and Cindy to Holiday next weekend, we'd love to have you. My folks would like to meet you. I promise it won't be too painful, and there will be loads of good food."

Levi offered her an astonished look, as though he hadn't expected the invitation and didn't quite know what to do with it. "May I get back to you with an answer?"

"Of course. You can let me know any time before we leave Friday afternoon. Cindy and I both got permission to leave work early. We plan to hit the road by three, which is only two at home since they're in the Pacific time zone."

Levi nodded and pointed out two deer standing at the edge of a creek. They drove for another hour, visiting like old friends, before he took a scrics of side roads and Grace could tell they were heading back toward Nampa.

"Are you up for dinner and a movie?" Levi asked as they neared town.

"Always, but I hope I'm not keeping you from work. I know you and your dad are so busy on the farm. I've taken up so much of your time today."

"It's fine, Grace. I put in extra hours all week so I could take today off. I need to check with Pop about being gone two Saturdays in a row, but it would be nice to meet your parents. I can't promise anything, but I will definitely consider going with you to Holiday."

"Excellent!" She sat back, dreaming of arriving in Holiday with a handsome man to escort her to Delia's wedding. She could almost see some of her cousins' faces turn green with envy. Not that she wanted Levi to go for that particular reason. She really wanted him to meet her parents and for her parents to meet the young man she couldn't seem to stop gushing about in her letters or Sunday night phone calls to them.

Levi was becoming more and more important to her, and she wanted her family to like him as much as she did.

"Have you ever eaten at Red Steer?" Levi asked as they drove through Nampa.

"A red steer? Isn't that what you raise? Herefords?"

Levi shook his head and pointed up the street to a white sign with a red steer head painted on it. "Not a red steer, *the* Red Steer."

"Nope. I don't know anything about the Red Steer."

Levi gave her a look like he might have given a child who'd announced they'd never heard of Santa Claus, then pulled into the parking lot of the drive-in and found a spot. They'd gone on enough dates, and spent enough time together, that he knew what she liked on her burger. When the waitress came over to take their order, Levi placed an order for two Ham'oneers, two orders of fries, and two milkshakes—one chocolate and one vanilla.

"What's a ham-o ... whatever it was you ordered?" Grace asked as the waitress hurried off to fill their order.

"Ham'oneer. It's a hamburger with this amazingly thick bacon on it that is like nothing else you've ever tasted." He offered her a teasing grin. "I left off the onions, though, in case you feel like having your way with me later."

"Well, thank you for that," Grace deadpanned, making Levi laugh.

When the food arrived, the hamburger was even better than she expected, and the chocolate shake was thick, creamy perfection on a warm summer afternoon.

After they finished eating, she dashed inside to use the restroom and wash up, then returned to the pickup to find Levi talking to two young men who appeared to be of a similar age. When one of them smiled and gave Levi's arm a playful swat with a ball cap, she assumed they were at least acquaintances, if not friends.

"Friends of yours?" she asked as she got in the pickup, and Levi started it.

"We competed against each other in high school. They graduated in Caldwell, but I knew them from sports and the county fair." He pulled onto the street and headed toward Boise. "Any movie you are interested in seeing?"

"No. I'm just happy to spend more time with you," Grace admitted. "I mean, someone has to keep a homely fellow like you company, and you are pretty generous with snacks and meals."

Levi lifted an eyebrow and pinned her with a steely look. "You keep tossing around compliments like that, and the snacks and meals might just disappear."

"Not that," Grace said, pretending to look repentant. "Don't take away my Ding Dongs and milkshakes!"

Levi laughed. "Okay. But only if you come sit a little closer instead of hanging out all the way over there."

Grace gladly moved close to him, breathing in his scent, resting in the comfort of his welcoming presence.

Fifteen minutes later, when he pulled into a drive-in movie, she couldn't resist clapping her hands in excited anticipation. "I haven't been to a drive-in for ages."

"Do you mind that it's a Bruce Lee movie?"

Grace shook her head. "I don't care what's playing. It's the experience that matters. Can we get popcorn? And a box of Whoppers?"

Levi grinned indulgently. "Whatever you want, Miss American Pie."

Grace frowned. "Is that going to be a thing now? You calling me that?"

"Maybe. Is that going to be a problem?"

"Maybe." She shrugged and started to scoot away from him, but he wrapped his hand around her waist and drew her close enough he could press a kiss to her neck, just below her ear. She giggled and squirmed, enjoying every second of his affection and attention.

It wasn't until they were parked and Levi had retrieved popcorn, candy, and two bottles of Dr Pepper from the concession stand that she noticed he watched her observantly. "Do you not like nicknames?"

"I don't mind them at all, Levi. I was just joking around earlier."

"I know, but I don't want to call you anything you don't like."

She didn't think he needed to know he could have called her "Hey, you," or "Mudface" and just hearing his voice would have sparked the same reaction she experienced every time he said *Grace* in that deep, rumbling voice she'd come to love.

"I'll let you know if you call me something I don't like," she said, then popped a Whopper in her mouth.

Grace paid far more attention to Levi than to the movie, but she enjoyed the evening immensely. The entire day had been wonderful, one she'd long remember.

When Levi finally drove her home and walked her inside, he gave her one knee-weakening kiss in front of the apartment door, squeezed her hand in his, kissed her cheek, and left.

Grace opened the apartment door and walked inside on wobbly legs, wondering how life could get any sweeter than it was at that very moment in time.

7

Levi walked along the aluminum sprinkler pipe in the potato field, checking to make sure the nozzles on each sprinkler head were clear and the pipes were connected. They'd irrigated the same way for as long as he could remember, using irrigation siphon tubes that carried water from the ditch down the furrows of soil.

When he returned home from Vietnam, he'd started studying new inventions and options for watering their crops. After much discussion, he'd talked his father into letting him purchase enough sprinkler pipe to test out a forty-acre field of potatoes. Levi anticipated the yield would noticeably increase due to having adequate water irrigate every plant instead of just those nearer the ditch or at the bottom of the field, where water sometimes tended to pool.

He bent down and pulled a kochia weed, carrying it with him. Gibson & Son Farms was known for their weed-free, well-tended fields, and Levi did all he could to maintain that. Anyone working on the farm knew to get a weed up by its roots instead of just breaking off the top. A cement-walled burn pit where they burned the weeds as well as trash was part of their efforts to keep invasive plants from spreading.

When Levi made it back to the top of the field, his left arm was loaded with weeds. He piled them into a bucket he'd strapped to the back of his Honda dirt bike. A scabbard attached to the side held a shovel, and a little toolbox was welded onto the back beneath the seat. He had everything he needed for making simple repairs in the field, or hauling out weeds, as the case was this morning.

Levi turned on the water to the sprinkler line, then watched to make sure each nozzle was spraying properly before he got on the bike, kick-started it, and moved on to the next field. It had been a challenge for him to learn to work the hand clutch on the bike with just his thumb and index finger on his left hand, but he'd managed. Now, he felt like those two digits were twice as strong as any of the fingers on his right hand.

Stubbornly, he refused to stop doing things he'd always done before the injury just because he was missing three fingers and a good portion of his hand. If there was a way for him to figure out how to make something work, he did.

He set the water in three more fields, checked on the cattle, fed the horses, and then headed to his parents' house for breakfast. Since he was doing more and more farm work, his mother insisted on feeding him breakfast and dinner. Most of the time, Levi went to his house and made a sandwich for lunch, needing an hour of quiet to settle himself before he returned to work.

Since meeting Grace almost two months ago, Levi felt as though his life had shifted yet again, except this time, it was in a better, more joyful direction. Honestly, since he'd met Grace, he'd been happier than he'd ever felt, even before he'd gone off to war.

Levi had been in love before, been engaged and then brokenhearted, but what he'd felt for Laurie seemed so insignificant compared to his growing feelings for Grace.

The moment he'd met Grace, she'd unsettled him, and it wasn't just about his fear of appearing weak in front of her. Part of what had left him so rattled was Grace. She was beautiful, of that there was no question. But she was also confident. Strong. Smart. Sweet. Funny. Interesting. Caring. Generous. And kind. She was so kind, and that was one of the things he loved most about her.

Levi wasn't sure of the exact moment he'd fallen in love with Grace. It might have been when she'd threatened him with the thermometer that first day in Dr. O'Brien's office, but he loved her with his whole heart. Loved her in a way that felt like it went down to the depths of his wounded soul.

Grace had filled his life with light and joy, and even hope, things that had been in short supply since he'd returned from the war.

Because of those precious gifts that she'd given him, he would have done anything for her in return.

Well, almost anything. Thursday, when he'd phoned to tell her he wouldn't be able to attend her cousin's wedding, she'd sounded so disappointed. He couldn't blame her. Part of him felt like the world's biggest heel for not going with her. After all, she'd been out to the farm on numerous occasions and had spent a considerable amount of time with his parents, particularly his mother.

Levi recalled a conversation he'd had with his mom just the other day.

"I like Grace, honey. She's the best thing that's ever happened to you, and she's not one of those idiotic girls who has no sense. She'll make a good wife and mother, and she fits right in here on the farm. You'd be a dunce if you let her get away," Stella Gibson had declared.

Levi had smirked at her as he leaned against the kitchen counter, drinking a glass of sweetened iced tea. "Isn't that basically what you said about Laurie? Look how that ended."

His mother had swatted him with a damp dish towel and scowled. "I never once said Laurie would make a good wife or mother. I said she was pretty and would make beautiful babies. Don't get smart with me, young man. You love Grace. I can see it on your face every time you mention her. You were never like this around Laurie. She did you a favor by breaking things off, that cruel ninny, because it left you free to find Grace. Your father and I both adore her, not that our opinions matter."

Levi had set his glass in the sink, then kissed his mother's cheek. "Your opinion does matter because if and when I do get around to marrying someone, they'll likely be living here on the farm. It is important to me that you not despise my future wife."

"Well, if you wise up and marry Grace, there won't be a problem. I couldn't love her anymore if she were my own daughter. Besides, she's much prettier than Laurie ever was. She's smart and witty, and the work she does means something, son. You won't find another girl just like Grace anywhere."

Levi knew his mother was right. Grace was one of a kind, and he'd likely never find anyone like her again.

It was because of how much he loved her that he hesitated to tell her his feelings, though. She was vibrant and full of life. He was battle-worn and damaged. She wanted to help save the world. He just wanted to escape from it.

Although he hadn't mentioned it to Grace, one of the many reasons he had been so quick to move out of his parents' home and into his own was because of his nightmares. Some nights he awakened screaming, drenched in sweat, thrashing around on the bed.

How could he subject Grace, or any woman, to that? What if he accidentally hit her or hurt her in his sleep? He wouldn't be able to live with himself if he did.

Levi hadn't returned to the farm the same innocent, stars-in-his-eyes boy he was when he left. He was a man who had seen too much pain and horror, and it haunted him, casting shadows across his soul and darkening the corners of his heart.

Because of that, because of his inability to look at his burned flesh and what was left of his hand without contempt and disgust, he knew he wasn't whole. So how could a less-than-whole man expect to marry an amazing, incredible woman like Grace Marshall?

He couldn't. That was the simple answer.

Yet, every time he thought about walking away from Grace, of never seeing her again, he felt sick inside. When he was with Grace, he could feel the light she brought into his life and heart, dispelling the lingering darkness.

Levi's mom and dad had encouraged him to go with Grace for the weekend. To meet her parents and see the small town where she'd grown up. Levi had waffled back and forth about going or staying home so many times in the past week he'd nearly given himself whiplash.

As much as he wanted to go with her, he feared taking that next step in their relationship. Meeting her family and childhood friends meant something. Something monumental. Something that alluded to future plans.

Plans he had not yet reconciled himself to making.

In the end, he'd chickened out and told Grace he couldn't go. He'd felt like a coward and the worst boyfriend in the world. All she'd asked of him, really the only thing she'd asked from him in their weeks together, was for him to go with her to the wedding.

And he'd let her down.

Plagued by guilt and burdened by the fear of losing her, Levi drove back to the house where he'd grown up, detouring on the way to dump the bucket of weeds into the burn pit.

When he stopped outside the big farmhouse, Spreckles barked and leaped off the porch, eager to greet him. The dog seemed to travel between his house and this one multiple times a day when she wasn't following him around on the farm.

He used the toe of his irrigating boot to push down the kickstand on the motorbike, then swung his leg over. Spreckles jumped up, and he caught her, laughing as she tried to lick his face. Her wiggly warmth made him smile, despite the turmoil roiling within him.

"Why are you here?" his mother shouted at him from the front door she yanked open. "Shouldn't you be on your way to Holiday?"

"Ma, I told you yesterday I wasn't going." Levi sighed and set the dog on her feet, then walked toward her. "It's better this way."

"Levi William Gibson, I did not raise you to be a coward. Grace has been nothing but kindness personified to you and to us. The least you can do is go to that wedding as her date. It's rude and … and …" Too exasperated for words, Stella stamped both feet as she stood on the front door mat. "You hightail it home and change, and then head to Holiday. If you hurry, you'll make it in time."

"Ma! I'm not going, and that is final. Leave it alone!" Levi bellowed, losing the tenuous hold he had on his temper. He felt a release as his anger came out to play.

His mother wasn't cowed in the least by his outburst, but it riled up his father who stepped outside drying his damp hands on a hand towel.

"Son, you apologize to your mother for raising your voice to her, or you and I are going to have a problem."

Contrition immediately settled over Levi. He never lost control like that. Never yelled, especially not at his parents. Never fought such an urge to pummel something.

Repentant, he took the porch steps in a few strides and offered his mother an apologetic look. "I'm sorry, Ma. I didn't mean to yell. I shouldn't have lost my temper."

"I know, honey." His mother patted his cheek. "I shouldn't push you so much."

"You both are right." Gary looked from his wife to his son. "I agree with your mother, though, Levi. You should either go to that wedding or break things off with Grace. If you don't care about that sweet, beautiful girl enough to attend the wedding and meet her folks, then you aren't that serious about her and should stop wasting her time."

Levi didn't like hearing his father's words of wisdom, even if he agreed with them. He felt like today was a pivotal point in his relationship with Grace. The choice he made was going to have a profound effect on their future.

Everything in him was shouting at him to rush to Holiday as quickly as he could get there. But the part of him that was afraid her family would measure him by his war wounds and find him lacking wanted to hide at home.

"Are you a man worthy of the love of a fine woman like Grace?" his father asked, his voice steady although his scowl deepened as he spoke.

The question goaded and pricked at Levi until he had to take a series of deep breaths to keep from shouting in anger again.

Rather than address the question of whether he would go or stay, he changed the subject. "You need help. I was gone all last Saturday as it was."

"You were, but you worked an extra ten hours during the week before then to make up for it, and you've been working twice as hard this week. We can manage for a day without you here. I know you don't want to hear what we have to say, son, but it's time to make a choice. Do you want to keep Grace or let her go? It is as simple and as complicated as that."

Levi could spend hours—days—searching his heart, weighing the pros and cons, and he knew the answer would be the same. He wanted Grace. Wanted a life with her. Wanted to love her with his whole heart.

Despite his mother's intrusiveness and his father's bluntness, they both were right. If he didn't go to this wedding, then he needed to walk away from Grace and set her free to find someone who would always be there for her.

The thoughts rolling around in his head must have shown on his face.

His father grinned and reached out to thump him on the back. "Hurry, son. You need to hurry."

Levi turned, tripped over the dog, and would have sprawled on his face if he hadn't latched onto the porch railing.

"Stop on your way out. I'll have a gift ready for the bride, and you should probably take one to Grace's parents."

"Right. Thanks, Ma! I'll pay you back."

"Yes, you will!" she called after him as he ran over to the motorbike, cranked it up, and made it back to his house in record time. He jerked off clothes as he entered through the back door, leaving them in a heap on the laundry room floor, then jumped into the shower and quickly shaved, only nicking himself once in the process.

He combed his hair, slapped on a little aftershave, then rushed to dress in a dark blue suit with a pale blue shirt. He grabbed a burgundy tie and shoved it in his pocket, tamped his feet into his best pair of cowboy boots, stuffed a white linen handkerchief in his back pants pocket, and tried to think if he'd forgotten anything.

After taking several bills from the stash of money he kept in a dresser drawer for emergencies, he slipped his checkbook into the inside pocket of his suitcoat and was almost out the door when he decided he should probably pack an overnight bag in case he decided to stay in Holiday. He grabbed his toiletry kit, dropped it in a duffel bag with a set of casual clothes, then grabbed a blue striped dress shirt, a dark blue tie, and a pair of tan trousers he could wear to church if he went with Grace tomorrow before coming home.

Assured he had what he needed, he removed the suit jacket and tossed it on the bag on his pickup seat, then sped to his parents' home. His mom ran out the door holding two gift-wrapped boxes in her hands before Levi made it all the way around the pickup. He opened the passenger door and greeted her with a smile.

"This one is for the bride and groom," she said, setting a box wrapped in white paper with a gold bow on top on the seat after she pushed his duffel bag on the floor and hung his suit jacket on the hook just inside the pickup door. "This is for Grace's parents." She placed a smaller box wrapped in blue and red plaid paper on top of his bag.

"Thanks, Ma. I appreciate it, and I'm really sorry about earlier."

"It's okay, honey." She gave him a big hug, then stepped back and offered him a critical look. "You look so handsome. Do you need help with your tie?"

"Yes, please." He tugged it out of his suit pocket, looped it around his neck, then lifted his chin. His mom had always tied his father's ties too. It seemed the Gibson men were all thumbs when it came to tying them properly.

"There," she said, loosening it so he could leave the top buttons of his shirt unfastened. "I hope you don't sweat clear through your clothes before you get there. It's warm today."

"It is, but I'll be fine." Levi glanced up as his father raced out of the house with a basket in one hand and an insulated thermos in the other.

"Here's some grub for the road. The thermos has ice water. There's also a bottle of pop in the basket." His father leaned into the pickup and set the basket where Levi could easily reach it.

Levi shook his father's hand, gave his mother one more hug, then slid behind the wheel and took off in a cloud of dust. According to his watch, he had four hours to get to Holiday in time for the wedding. That should be plenty enough time to arrive, as long as he didn't have any trouble along the way.

8

"Are you still moping?" Cindy asked as she and Grace got ready for Delia's wedding in Cindy's childhood bedroom.

Grace's parents' home was overrun with relatives in town for the wedding, so she'd retreated to the calm and quiet of Cindy's house.

Grace bent her knees to look into the mirror and applied one last brush of the soft rose-hued lipstick she'd worn since she'd discovered it four years ago. It was perfect for her skin tone, and it lasted better than any other product she'd ever tried. She glanced at Cindy as her friend sat on the vanity stool in front of the dressing table mirror, applied a coat of Tangee lipstick, and smacked her lips together to rub in the coloring.

"I am not moping," Grace said, adjusting a stray lock of hair in the back of Cindy's hairstyle. Her friend had doused her hair with a liberal coating of Sun In, and the smell hadn't fully dissipated. She had no idea why Cindy insisted on using the odorous product when her hair always lightened naturally in the summer months anyway.

"Just because Levi couldn't come this weekend doesn't mean anything. As you know, summer is the busiest time of year for farmers."

"I know," Grace snapped, then sighed. "Sorry. It's just I so wanted him to come, to meet everyone and them to meet him. I know he's busy and couldn't get away, but still, I …"

"Wanted to show him off?" Cindy asked with a teasing grin. "He's not too ugly, at least for an unsophisticated farm boy, and he's not entirely dumb or completely unable to carry on a conversation."

Grace glanced in the mirror, making a face as she placed her hands at Cindy's throat, pretending to throttle her.

Both girls laughed.

"Seriously, Grace, he's pretty wonderful. Not only is he handsome, but he also has that boyish charm thing going for him. He's smart and funny and a lot of fun. I like him, and not just for him. I like him for you. When you're with him, you seem like the very best version of yourself. When he's around, you're so happy it would be utterly disgusting under other circumstances."

Grace hugged Cindy's shoulders and straightened. "I just wish he could have been here, not because I want to show him off, which we both know that I do. It's because I wanted him to see Holiday and meet my family and know where I came from, if that makes any sense."

"It does." Cindy rose from the stool and turned to Grace. "We might have to skimp on our grocery budget the rest of the month, but these dresses are worth it."

The yellow polka-dotted dress with puffed sleeves and a lace bib on the front was perfect for Cindy's complexion and hair color.

Grace smoothed her hand along the front of her cream cotton dress overlaid with sheer fabric featuring teal velvet roses. A teal velvet ribbon tied into a bow at the front of her waist, with the streamers ending just above the skirt's deep flounce. A ruffled, rounded neckline and sheer sleeves with a tight six-inch button placket at the wrist made her feel feminine and pretty. She and Cindy had both opted for wedge sandals, so they could dance as long as they liked in stylish comfort.

"Come on. We don't want to be late," Grace said, adjusting a wayward curl. She'd spent the morning with her hair wrapped around big pink foam curlers, then swept the curls away from her face in a style she hoped closely copied one she'd seen Raquel Welch sporting in a recent magazine article.

Quickly stuffing a few essentials into handbags, they rushed downstairs.

"See you at the church," Cindy called to her parents, who were in the kitchen, then she and Grace hurried outside and headed down the tree-lined sidewalk toward the Holiday Community Church, where the wedding would take place.

Even though Grace wasn't part of the wedding party, she'd offered to arrive early to help with anything that was needed. Of course, Cindy had also offered her assistance.

They arrived at the church to find the florist was running late and hastened to help set out the flowers when they arrived. From there, they'd answered questions from early guests, checked on the bride and declared her beyond gorgeous, chased two ornery boys away from the guest book, then finally went to find seats.

She and Cindy had just walked into the back of the church when Grace was jostled and bumped into by the person behind her. She turned to apologize, only to have her jaw drop open in shock.

Levi smiled down at her, and her heart felt like it sprouted wings and soared right out of her chest. Up until that moment, she hadn't allowed herself to acknowledge how desperately she'd wanted him there beside her.

"Hi, stranger," she said, leaning against him so she could speak in his ear above the din of the growing crowd.

"Hi, Miss American Pie." He kissed her cheek, then blushed as he noticed several people staring at them.

"I'm so glad you're here." Grace laced their fingers together and led him to the pew where Cindy had taken a seat by Grace's brothers. Micah was threatening to mess up Jason's combed hair, while Cindy lectured them both on behaving in the church.

"Levi Gibson, I'd like you to meet my brothers. Micah is the old one wearing a scowl. Jason has his tie on crooked," she said with a mocking smile, then playfully tugged on Jason's tie.

Levi grinned and shook hands with both of them, then waited for Grace to take a seat by Cindy before settling on the end of the pew nearest the wall.

When Micah winked at Grace, she knew her big brother approved of her choice of a boyfriend. In fact, other than the boys she'd dated in school, whom her family all knew, Levi was the first boyfriend she'd invited home to meet them.

Still taken aback by his unexpected appearance, she leaned closer to him. "I thought you couldn't make it."

He shrugged and slipped his right arm around her shoulders. "I decided here with you was where I needed to be. I hope it's okay that I came."

"Better than okay," she whispered, looking up at him, wishing they were alone so he'd kiss her instead of in a church surrounded by people she'd known her whole life who would not only observe but discuss, at length, her every move since she'd brought a stranger into their midst.

She rested against Levi, grateful for the contentment she found in his presence. His minty breath blew warm across her cheek, and she shifted her head slightly to look up at him.

"You look like a princess in that pretty dress, Grace."

"Thank you, kind sir. You look quite dashing in that suit." She adjusted his tie slightly, then patted his chest before settling back against him.

The wedding music began, and the ceremony proceeded smoothly. When Grace sniffled as the couple exchanged vows, Levi handed her a snowy white handkerchief. She dabbed at her eyes and nose, then clutched the linen square, breathing deeply of Levi's scent. Unless she surprised him at the farm when he was dirty and sweating as he worked in the fields, he always smelled so good.

She couldn't believe he drove all the way to Holiday just to attend the wedding with her, but she was beyond thankful that he had. With him there, everything that had seemed wrong before now suddenly seemed so right.

Throughout the afternoon reception, she introduced Levi to relatives, friends, and even her fourth-grade teacher, who was related to the groom on his mother's side. She excused herself to the powder room and was on her way to find Levi when she heard her mother speaking to her long-time best friend.

"I could hardly believe it, Janie. She's never been like this about anyone before. I hate to think I might lose my little girl, but he seems like a wonderful young man, so polite and smart. Did I tell you his family has a potato farm? Four generations, I think Gracie said. I think he comes from a solid family, and I'm so pleased for Gracie."

Delighted her mother approved of Levi, Grace returned to find him speaking with Micah and her father. She edged around them to listen to Levi asking questions about their dairy, a favorite topic of both her father and her brother, and answering their queries about growing potatoes and sugar beets.

Grace knew her father could talk farming for hours without coming up for air, so she interrupted them, grabbed Levi's hand, and tugged him toward the dance floor. Although he claimed to have two left feet, he could hold his own, and she'd thoroughly enjoyed dancing with him. Levi tended to want to stay where he could see the exit or have his back to the wall, but other than that, he seemed to have fun.

By the time the evening ended and they'd tossed handfuls of rice at the departing newlyweds, Grace was ready for some peace and quiet, not to mention food. Between helping where she was needed and trying to keep her relatives from relentlessly interrogating Levi, she didn't get a chance to eat more than a handful of cocktail peanuts, and a few of the pastel buttermints served in crystal dishes on the end of the cake table.

Levi removed his suit jacket and joined the men in putting away chairs and tables while the women washed dishes and tidied the kitchen.

Grace was wiping off a counter when Cindy bumped her with her elbow. "Get out of here and take that hunky fella of yours for something to eat. Cake and peanuts aren't enough to sustain a growing boy, you know."

"I'm hungrier than he is. He at least got cake," Grace joked, then handed the dishcloth to Cindy. "If anyone asks, we're going to get dinner, and then I'll be back at the house."

Before anyone else waylaid her, Grace rushed out of the kitchen in the church's basement to find Levi helping carry gifts out to her aunt and uncle's car. The happy couple would open them when they returned from their honeymoon in California. They'd decided to go camping in the redwood forest, which did not sound like fun to Grace, but she hoped they enjoyed it.

When Levi set a box in the trunk and turned around, Grace held up his suit jacket and tipped her head toward the church parking lot. He grinned and hurried toward her, taking her hand in his as they walked over to his pickup.

Once he'd seated her and slid behind the wheel, he gave her a long look. "You really are beautiful, Miss American Pie."

"Thank you, Levi, and thank you for being here. It means so much."

He gently squeezed her fingers, then started the pickup. "Where to?"

"I'm starving. We can get burgers and take them out to the lake. I know just the spot to eat them."

"Just tell me where to go."

Two hours later, after they'd watched the sunset from the dock at the lake, toes trailing in the water, and kissed so many times Grace felt both euphoric and lightheaded, Levi drove her home.

"Do you want to stay here tonight? We could find room for you somewhere."

"I think I'd better head on home, but I had an amazing time with you today, Grace, and I really like your family. Jason is a kick in the pants, and Micah is really cool."

"I'm glad you like them, Levi. If you detested them, would you tell me the truth?"

He looked her in the eye and nodded. "I would. You have a great family. I enjoyed talking farming with your dad. I see your classic beauty comes from your mom."

Grace smiled, wondering how Levi always seemed to know just the right thing to say. "Are you sure you won't stay? I hate to think of you making that long drive in the dark. What if you hit a deer or something?"

"I'll be fine, but thanks for worrying about me." He got out of the pickup and walked around it, opening the door for her. He took a small box from the seat next to her, tucked it under his left arm, then took her left hand with his right. "Would it be okay if I said goodbye to your parents?"

"Of course. They'll like that."

Grace led the way into the house and found her mom and dad in the kitchen, eating ice cream and leftover cake with Micah. Jason had taken the rest of their houseguests for a drive and hadn't yet returned.

"You're just in time for dessert," Grace's mother said as she and Levi walked into the room. Before her mother could rise to serve them, Grace hurried to set slices of cake on plates and added generous scoops of ice cream. She carried them to the table, poured two glasses of iced tea, then sat down next to her mom, leaving Levi to sit between her and Micah.

"This is delicious," Levi said, dabbing at his mouth with a napkin Grace had handed to him from the basket in the center of the table.

"We're glad you could make the trip up here today, Levi," her father said with a friendly smile, one Grace knew was genuine. "Tell me more about that new sprinkler system you mentioned."

Grace tried not to roll her eyes as her father and Micah talked farming with Levi. She cleared away the empty dishes, setting them in the portable dishwasher with a butcher block top, refilled tea glasses, then gave her mother a look that caused her to smile in understanding.

"You can talk farming another day, Mike," Jo-Ann Marshall declared to her husband. "Let the poor boy get on the road before it gets any later."

"You sure we can't talk you into staying, Levi?" Mike asked. "If you'd be more comfortable, there's a hotel in town. It's a little run down, but the rooms are clean."

Levi glanced at Grace, and she poured all of her silent pleading for him to stay into that one look. He winked at her and nodded his head. "I suppose I could stay one night, but I'll get a room at the hotel."

After he thanked her parents for their hospitality, she walked with him out to his pickup, kissing his cheek since Jason pulled up with a carload of relatives, stealing what moments of privacy they may have had.

"Come for breakfast, and then we can go to church together."

"I'll see you then, Grace." Levi squeezed her hand before he got into the pickup and drove off, taking her heart along for the ride.

9

"Ma! You do know you don't have to feed everyone all by yourself, don't you?" Levi asked as he packed a huge platter full of sliced watermelon out to the tables set up in their backyard.

Every Fourth of July, his parents hosted a barbecue for his mother's relatives. To Levi, it seemed like she had hordes of them, but for the most part, he'd enjoy the day. Everyone would arrive shortly before noon, and they'd eat until they felt like their stomachs would burst from all the good food. After lounging around for an hour and visiting, anyone who wanted could join in a baseball game held in the pasture, where there was no chance of a stray ball breaking a window.

He and his dad had spent part of the morning setting up tables and chairs. Levi had cleaned up the baseball equipment and hauled it out to the pasture, which he'd mowed with the swather last week.

The past few days, his mother had nearly run his legs off, asking him and his dad and some of their hired hands to help get the place "ready for company," as she called it. They'd hosed off the outside of all the buildings, washed windows, and mowed the lawn and edged it, all while Stella Gibson had barked orders like a general in the Army. When she wasn't in the kitchen cooking for the holiday, she was pointing out where she wanted new plants placed or mapping out the exact location for the tables and chairs set around the backyard.

Grace had come out yesterday when she'd gotten off work and helped Levi hang patriotic bunting along the front and back porches. She'd even helped his mother make flower arrangements for the tables and offered a few ideas for additional decorations.

Levi was excited to spend the day with her, and he was glad she'd talked Cindy into coming along. Since the holiday fell in the middle of the week, the girls didn't want to try to make a quick trip to Holiday. Levi was more than happy to invite them to join in his family's day of festivities.

When he heard gravel crunch, he jogged around the corner of the house and waved as Grace parked her car down by the barn, out of the way. She and Cindy hopped out, each of them carrying food as they headed toward him.

Levi waited at the edge of the yard, savoring the opportunity to watch Grace move. She was, as her name implied, full of grace. Today, she wore a navy and white polka-dot mini dress nipped in at the waist with a red belt. As she walked, though, he realized the slits in the front of the skirt were to show off a pair of red and white polka-dot shorts worn beneath the top.

Her luxurious brown hair bounced in curls cascading from the top of her head where she'd pinned it.

"Pie!" he called, making her roll her eyes and Cindy laugh.

Cindy held up a pie dish. "How did you know I was making a strawberry pie?" she teased, fully aware he referred to Grace by the abbreviated nickname he'd given to her. Sometimes he called her Pie, other times, it was Meripie. Often, it was Miss American Pie, but it was always said with love.

His attendance at her cousin's wedding a few weeks ago had shifted something between the two of them. It was as though the effort he'd made to be there for her and the approval he'd received from her family had somehow deepened and strengthened their relationship.

Levi still had no idea what his future might hold, especially when it came to Grace, but he'd decided for now to enjoy a summer of being in love. Of holding a beautiful girl in his arms, his heart, and his dreams and not worrying about what would happen later.

Today was more than enough.

"Hi," Grace said, leaning in to kiss his cheek.

At the last second, Levi turned his head so the kiss landed right on his lips.

Grace blushed as she stepped back, aware of his parents watching them from a distance.

"What did you bring?" he asked, looking at the plate she held covered by a tall cake dome.

"Sock-it-to-me cake."

"A whozeewhatzit cake?" he asked, pretending not to understand her.

Grace elbowed him in the side, making him grunt with feigned injury. "I found the recipe in a magazine last week. I don't know where the name came from, but it's basically a buttery Bundt cake with pecans and a caramel swirl, topped with more caramel glaze and nuts. I seem to recall someone around here has a fondness for pecans."

"Buttering up my dad won't earn you any favors," he said with a sardonic grin. "Then again, maybe it will."

Grace laughed and greeted his mom with a warm one-armed hug. He was glad to see Cindy speaking to his father, showing she felt at ease there. She'd been out with Grace a few times, and the girls had gone to church with them and stayed for lunch last Sunday. Levi had loved sitting through the church service with Grace beside him, although her alluring fragrance combined with her appealing presence had made it hard for him to concentrate on the sermon.

"I love your outfit, Grace. Is it new?" Stella asked as she took the cake plate from her and set it on a table designated for desserts.

"I made it. Cindy and I found a great sale on material, and I had the pattern from some my aunt had given to me."

"It looks so cute and perfect for Independence Day."

Levi watched his mother rush to greet the first of her family to arrive. He walked over to Grace, looping an arm around her waist. When she leaned back against him, he pressed a light kiss to her neck. "I'm so glad you're here, Grace."

"Me too, Levi."

Once the relatives all arrived, Levi felt like he didn't get a minute to spend with Grace. His mother had him manning the barbecue grill, cooking burgers and frankfurters as fast as he could for what seemed like hundreds of people, but was probably closer to forty.

When the afternoon segued to the baseball game, Levi planned to find some reason not to participate, partially because of his hand but mostly because he wanted to be with Grace.

He was shocked to discover both she and Cindy had volunteered to play on his dad's team.

"Oh, it's on now, Meripie!" He waggled a finger at her, and everyone laughed.

Levi hadn't tried to play baseball since he'd returned from the war, but he figured the worst that could happen was he'd strike out. When it was his turn to bat, he had to adjust his stance and grip on the bat, but he managed to hit the ball on the second swing, and it sailed out toward center field.

"Run!" he yelled to his uncle on third base as he headed to first.

The game was lively, and Grace and Cindy joined his cousins in lobbing taunting comments at him, but it was all in good fun. He dished out the jibes as fast as he received them.

When the game ended with his dad's team winning, Levi cheered along with everyone else, mostly because Grace and Cindy were so thrilled with their victory.

After his aunts and mother hauled out gallons of homemade ice cream in four different flavors, they all ate until their brains felt frozen. Eventually, many of them participated in games of horseshoes, darts, three-legged races, and even a water balloon toss. Dinner was one of Levi's favorite meals all year. His mother and aunts served baked beans, roasted potatoes, corn on the cob, and a pit-smoked pig that Levi and his father had been cooking since the previous evening. The meat was so tender and flavorful, it almost melted on his tongue.

Bellies full and children sleepy, everyone packed up and headed home, but only after everything had been set to rights in the yard and kitchen.

Levi's parents, exhausted from the long day, sank onto the couch in the living room with their feet propped up and dozed. Normally, they would take a rest, then the three of them would drive into town to watch a fireworks display.

This year, though, Levi had invited Grace and Cindy to go with him to one of the local auto raceways for a drag race followed by a big fireworks extravaganza, or so the newspaper article had said. He'd purchased the tickets in advance so they wouldn't have to worry about getting in.

While Grace and Cindy took a few minutes to clean up and rest, Levi retreated to his old bedroom and took a quick shower, trading the tank top and cut-off shorts he'd worn all day for a pair of jeans and a red, white, and blue plaid western shirt.

He settled his straw hat on his still-wet head, then went to the kitchen, where the girls sat at the table drinking glasses of ice water.

"Are you ready to go?" he asked, tamping his feet into his cowboy boots.

Grace's hair was no longer confined on top of her head. Instead, it fell around her shoulders in chunky curls. Levi wanted to wrap the spirals around his fingers, let the strands trail up his arms, and bury his nose in the decadent tropical scent of it, but there would be time for a few stolen kisses and moments with her later.

Tonight, he wanted to make sure Grace and Cindy had fun. Because the day had been so warm and it hadn't yet cooled off, his mother had insisted he take her car because it had air-conditioning. Under other circumstances, he would have declined and driven his pickup, but her car would be far more comfortable both because of the back seat for Cindy to ride in and the cool air that would be welcome in the summer's heat. He snagged the keys from a little gold hook by the wall telephone in the kitchen and opened the back door.

"I'm calling shotgun," Cindy teased as she raced out the door ahead of Grace.

"Should I be worried?" Levi asked as he and Grace walked hand in hand down the steps and over to the car.

"Nope." Grace bumped her hip against his as they walked, and he knew happiness beyond anything he'd ever experienced.

Maybe there was a chance for them. If he could get his night terrors under control, and could get past his injuries, then maybe a possibility existed that he and Grace could have a future together.

When they reached the car, he started it and adjusted the cool air setting to high, letting the warm air blow through the vents before they got in.

It didn't take long for the car to cool down and they were soon on their way to the raceway.

As they arrived and pulled into a long line of vehicles seeking parking, Levi felt his tension rising. Grace placed her hand on his arm and he instantly felt calmer. He finally found a parking place that wouldn't require a mile-long hike in the heat to reach the raceway. On the way to their seats, he stopped and bought bottles of icy cold soda, a box of popcorn, and another of salted peanuts.

Their seats were at the end of a row near the middle of the track, where they'd have a good view of the cars. Levi had purposely chosen seats at the back of a section so no one would be immediately behind him. It made him nervous to be around big crowds of strangers.

Although he'd experienced plenty of nerves at Grace's cousin's wedding, it was a different type of nervousness, borne from meeting her family and seeing her hometown more so than being in an unfamiliar and unsettling setting.

Levi drew in several deep breaths, trying to block out as much noise as possible. He listened to

Grace and Cindy discuss the various cars that were pulling out onto the track and their excitement about the fireworks show afterward.

Levi had always loved watching fireworks displays. In fact, when he was sixteen, he and two of his buddies had pooled their money and purchased a huge box full of them. Unfortunately, a few fireworks had gone awry and set his friend's father's dry wheat field ablaze. After that fiasco and the fear of being unable to put out a fire before it consumed a season's crop, Levi had left detonating fireworks to the professionals and gone into town to watch the show with his parents.

"Right, Levi?" Grace asked, drawing him back to the moment and her conversation with Cindy.

"I missed what you said, Grace. I'm sorry."

"I was just telling Cindy about our plans to go fishing next weekend. Didn't you say there would be trout?"

He nodded. "You're welcome to come along, Cindy. I can fill a can of worms just for you."

Cindy wrinkled her nose and tossed him a look of revulsion. "No, thank you. A day spent putting slimy things on hooks to pull slimy things out of stinky water in the broiling July heat is not my idea of a good time, but thanks for offering."

Levi chuckled. "You sure know how to suck the fun right out of an outdoorsy adventure."

"Perhaps we should go shopping instead," Grace said with mock seriousness.

Levi groaned in misery. "Not that. Why would you punish me like that? Haven't I already served my shopping sentence time for the year?"

"You were pretty handy to have around that day at the mall, especially with Tommy and Rick." Cindy leaned around Grace to grin at him. "The boys were asking about you when I saw them Sunday afternoon."

"Maybe the next time I'm over at your apartment, I'll pop by and swap howdies with them."

Grace giggled. "If you add a little more drawl to your voice, Tex, the boys will think you've walked right out of a set for western television show."

Before Levi could reply, the first race of the evening was announced. The odors of exhaust and burning rubber blended with dust, sweat, popcorn, and cotton candy in a confusing mixture of smells.

Levi scooted closer to Grace, slipped his arm around her, and breathed deeply of her pineapple fragrance. With it filling his nose and her close to his side, he was able to block out the noise of the crowd and focus on the cars racing.

As the evening faded into darkness and the lights around the track came on, the announcer concluded the races for the evening and announced the winners. Prizes were given, then the track was cleared, and the fireworks show began.

At first, it was the kind of fireworks any kid could pick up at the corner store. Then the explosions grew higher and louder.

Levi's ears began to ring as the smell of gunpowder and smoke assaulted his nostrils. When one of the fireworks emitted a shrill whistle before exploding with a thunderous boom, he felt like he'd fallen back into a war zone. Heat consumed him as he yanked open the snaps on his shirt and fanned his cowboy hat in front of his face, desperate to cool off as a woozy feeling settled over him. The fireworks faded in the distance until his mind convinced him he was no longer at the raceway but back in Vietnam in the midst of a battle zone. Blackness seeped into him until he couldn't see anything but darkness.

"Levi?" He could hear Grace's voice from what seemed miles away.

"Levi!" she called again, but he couldn't get to her. He was too lost in the terror of his past to return to the present.

10

"You! Will you help us? Please?" Grace motioned to two young men seated across the row from where she sat with Cindy and Levi.

The day had been filled with joy and fun, and the evening at the raceway, watching cars drag race had been something new and exciting.

She hadn't given a thought to Levi experiencing a problem with the fireworks, and neither had he. But she knew the minute something was wrong. He'd pulled away from her and placed his hands over his ears. Then he'd looked like he might be sick before he ripped his shirt open and fanned his face with his hat.

He got a faraway look in his eyes and slumped in his seat, like he'd blacked out. There was no possibility she and Cindy could get him out of the stands without help, but he needed to leave immediately.

Grace had seen this type of reaction to stimulus many, many times at the hospital. It could be a sound or a smell or even the sight of something that would cause a soldier to relive a traumatic moment from his time at war.

They needed to get Levi out of the stands. When he came to, he might still think he was in Vietnam and defend himself. If he were cognizant of his surroundings, she had no doubt he'd be mortified at what had happened.

Despite what he was likely to think, people were too involved in watching the fireworks to pay any attention to them.

"Please?" she pleaded with the two men, desperate to get Levi somewhere quiet where he'd feel safe.

The two young men stood and hurried over.

"Did he have too much to drink?" one of them asked as he got on one side of Levi while his friend moved to take a position on his other.

"No. He's a war veteran and is experiencing a flashback. I just need to get him away from the noise."

"Yes, ma'am," the two men said, hauling Levi to his feet between them. As they made their way out of the stands, the fireworks display turned from amazing to spectacular, keeping the attention of those around them on the sky instead of the five people rushing out of the stands, one of them unconscious.

"Thank you, Lord," Grace muttered as she and Cindy led the way to Stella's car. She fished into Levi's pocket and found the keys, unlocked the doors, and had the men settle Levi in the back seat.

She got in and started the car, letting welcome, cool air fill it as she quickly debated the best course of action. Levi needed to go home. Immediately. Was it safer for her to drive since Cindy rarely did and never at night? Or was it better to take their chances with Cindy puttering along behind the wheel while Grace sat in the back with Levi in case he came to before they got him home?

Grace decided it would be far faster for her to drive. If Levi woke up thinking he was still in a war zone, hopefully, she could talk him out of it.

"What can I do?" Cindy asked as she looked over the front passenger seat at Levi's prone form sprawled across the back seat.

"Pray." Grace buried her foot in the accelerator and hoped she wouldn't get a speeding ticket between the raceway and the farm.

Amazingly, no one pulled her over as she made it back to Star in half the time it had taken them to get to the raceway. Rather than take Levi to his house, she drove directly to his parents' home. The lights were all off, but she knew Levi shouldn't be alone.

She pulled the car around by the end of the front walk and slid to a stop.

"Cindy, run get Gary, please. We'll need his help getting Levi out of the car."

Cindy raced down the walk, bounded up the porch steps, and pounded on the door while ringing the bell incessantly. The porch light had been left on, but lights began clicking on throughout the house, and the door swung open. Gary rubbed sleep from his eyes, wearing a pair of plaid shorts and a white T-shirt. Stella rushed up behind him with her housecoat snapped crooked, the hem hanging at a crazy angle, and wire mesh rollers poking out from beneath a silk scarf she'd tied around her head.

"It's Levi," Grace heard Cindy explain, then the three people on the porch ran to the car door that she'd opened.

Levi looked like he was in a trance, with his eyes rapidly moving behind his closed lids. His body twitched, and he moaned. His right hand batted at something only he could see. His muscles bunched, tense and tight, as though he prepared to defend himself.

"Levi. You're safe. You're home. Everything is fine," Grace muttered as she climbed on the other side of him, hoping she could help push him out far enough they could get him on his feet and into the house.

It took the work of all four of them to get him out of the car and into the bed in his childhood bedroom.

Stella went to get a cool cloth and a glass of water while Gary pulled off Levi's boots. Cindy hung the straw hat she'd rescued from the bleachers on the rung of a desk chair, then left to help Stella.

Grace had shifted from girlfriend to nurse the moment she'd sensed Levi was in distress. Not giving a thought to anything but helping him, she had Gary hold him while she removed his shirt, then they worked off his jeans. She was grateful Levi wasn't the type of guy to forego underwear, or the situation could have turned extremely embarrassing for all of them.

Together, she and Gary tucked him in beneath a crisp cotton sheet that smelled of sunshine and laundry soap.

"He won't want you here when he comes out of this," Gary said softly as he adjusted the covers over Levi.

"I know, but I'd like to stay a few minutes, just to make sure he'll be okay." Grace feathered her fingers through his thick hair. His skin didn't feel nearly as hot as it had earlier. He wasn't moving around as much, either. His eyes no longer darted around behind his lids, which was a good sign.

She looked up at Gary as he stood on the other side of the bed. "Has this happened before?"

"Not that I'm aware of, in a public place, I mean. He has nightmares, night trauma might be a better description. When he was living here after he came back, he would wake us up shouting and yelling, and it would take hours for the tremors to stop. It bothered him that we saw him that way. He sees it as a weakness. I tried to talk to him about it, but he refuses to listen or discuss it. I know that's why he wanted to move into my brother's old house, to fight his demons alone."

"He hates to show anything he sees as weakness," Grace said, sitting on the edge of the mattress and taking the cool cloth Stella handed to her when she hurried into the room. Grace noticed Cindy chose to remain elsewhere, which was for the best. The fewer people around, the easier it would be on Levi when he did awaken.

Grace sponged his face, neck, chest, and hands, then Stella went to rinse it out with cool water. Although there was a bathroom in Levi's room, Stella headed to the kitchen in her unsettled state.

Grace took Levi's pulse and found it to be normal. His breathing was even and steady now, and she was sure he had actually gone to sleep.

"I think he'll be fine the rest of the night. I could sit with him if you'd like me to," Grace volunteered, hoping Gary and Stella wouldn't think her forward for offering. She needed to be with Levi, not as a nurse watching over a patient, but as a woman needing to be near the man she loved.

"No, Grace. You have to work tomorrow, don't you? We'll keep an eye on him." Gary patted her on the shoulder. "You and Cindy should go home."

Grace gently brushed her fingers through Levi's hair again, kissed his cheek, and whispered, "I love you, Levi," in his ear, then rose from the bed.

Stella rushed in with the cool cloth and, after handing it to Gary, gave Grace a tight hug. "Thank you for getting him home safely, darling. I'll phone you in the morning and let you know how he's doing."

"I'd appreciate that, Stella. Thank you." Grace kissed the woman's soft cheek, dodging to miss being poked in the eye with a hair roller, then left the room. She longed to stay beside Levi until she could talk to him and reassure him everything was fine, but Gary was correct. It would bother Levi more if she was there than if he only had to face his parents when he awakened.

Grace had no idea about his night trauma or the triggers that would set him off. Obviously, Levi had done a good job of covering up his problems, perhaps even from himself.

There were several excellent physicians at the hospital who could help him if he'd let them. But the first step was going to be Levi admitting he had a problem and needed help.

Grace found Cindy in the kitchen, mindlessly eating a piece of apple pie. Cindy shoved the last bite in her mouth and hugged Grace around the shoulders, and the two of them walked out to where Grace had parked her car that morning when the day had been so full of happiness and anticipation.

Silently, they drove back to their apartment, took turns showering, and climbed into bed.

Grace thought Cindy had gone to sleep, but in the darkness, she felt the mattress dip and Cindy wrap her arms around her.

"It's going to be okay, Grace. Everything will be okay." Then Cindy returned to her room, leaving Grace alone with her thoughts.

The entire day played over in her mind. She'd been shocked to arrive and find Levi wearing cut-off shorts that hit just above his knees, tennis shoes, which she didn't even know he owned, and a tank top with a stylish pair of aviator sunglasses. Pride had filled her at Levi's willingness to let his extended family see the healing scars on his arm. The whole bunch of Stella's relatives had moved up a notch in Grace's esteem as they'd all treated Levi no differently than anyone else despite his war wounds.

There had been so much food, more than she thought she'd ever seen on a table, and they'd eaten until she'd been sure she'd never want to eat again. Grace had met many of the relatives on previous occasions, but seeing them all together and the playful teasing way they interacted had reminded her of her own relatives. Oddly enough, instead of making her homesick, it had made her feel comforted to be around a welcoming, fun-loving group of people who had gone out of their way to include her and Cindy.

After the baseball game, there had been more time for visiting as they'd indulged in dessert. Grace hated to think about all the sweets and ice cream she'd eaten.

Levi had raved about her cake and had even taken a piece to his father, who also seemed to like it, if the two subsequent pieces he'd eaten were any indication. It had made her feel good that she'd contributed something the two Gibson men enjoyed.

After a delicious dinner that was unlike anything she'd ever experienced, they'd headed to the raceway. Drag races weren't something Grace had ever even thought of watching, but she and Cindy had enjoyed the novelty of it. If only they'd left at the end of the races instead of staying for the fireworks. Grace should have considered the possibility of them triggering Levi, but he'd never given even a hint that he struggled with any lingering issues from his time in Vietnam.

She realized Levi's scars went far deeper than those she could see. Likely, there were layers of them that would haunt him until he took them out and dealt with them in the open. Shoving them into the corners of his mind wasn't going to make the problems go away. It would only make matters worse.

How could she make him understand that it wasn't a sign of weakness to seek help, but rather one of strength?

Tossing and turning most of the night, when Grace did sleep, her dreams were full of nightmares of Levi calling out to her for help and being unable to reach him.

At four, she awakened drenched in sweat and knew she wouldn't go back to sleep. As quietly as possible, she got up and showered, dressed for work, and wrote Cindy a note explaining where she'd gone. She added an apology for not being there to drive her to the hospital. She suggested Cindy call and ask for a ride from one of the women who worked in the administrative office and lived just a few blocks up the street.

Grace tossed an apple, crackers, and cheese into a brown bag for her lunch, snagged a breakfast bar to eat on her way to the Gibson's farm, and left at five-thirty.

Normally, she would never arrive at someone's home so early in the day, but she knew the Gibson family were early risers. Levi was often out working by five in the morning.

When she pulled up at the farmhouse, it wasn't quite yet six, but the house was ablaze with light.

Levi's pickup was where he'd parked it the previous day, so Grace knew he was at the house.

Before she could go to work, she needed to see for herself that he was okay. As she made her way down the walk, Spreckles rose from the rug where she'd slept by the door. The dog stretched, then waggled her back end as Grace gave her a few affectionate pats before she knocked on the door.

She only had to wait a few seconds for the door to open and Gary to step back, motioning her inside.

"I thought I saw your car pull up," he said in almost a whisper.

"Is something wrong?" she asked, feeling the tension in the air around her.

"It's Levi. He finally woke up around four and has been ..." Gary sighed and ran a hand through his disheveled hair. The poor man looked like he hadn't slept a wink all night. He was dressed in jeans and a cotton work shirt, but concern furrowed his brow, and a muscle in his jaw tightened just like Levi's did whenever he was upset. "Maybe it would be best if you go."

"What's wrong, Gary? If there is something I can do to help Levi, I'd like to try."

"He's not in a good place right now, Grace. In fact, I've never seen him like this."

Grace frowned. "Do we need to take him to the hospital?"

"He seems fine as far as physical problems go, but he's ..." Gary paused again, and a sound from the hallway drew their gazes to Levi.

If Grace didn't know it was her Levi, she wasn't sure she'd recognize him. His hair stood straight up on end. His skin looked ashen, with dark circles beneath his eyes. He appeared both livid and humiliated. He wore only a pair of jeans, and she could see how his shoulders were pulled up so high with tautness, they practically crowded his ears.

On any other day, she might have made a joke to tease him into a better mood, but she knew instinctively Levi wouldn't stand for it. Not now.

"Go!" Levi shouted, pointing toward the door. "Now!"

Grace stood her ground. "No."

Stella raced out from the kitchen, her normally coiffed hair in wild disarray, eyes wide and full of fear.

"I said go, Grace. I don't need you here. I don't want you here." Levi lifted a trembling hand and pointed toward the door again. "Haven't you seen enough to know it's time to walk away from this?"

She shook her head, unwilling to accept what he was saying. "You need help, Levi. I want to help you. We all do."

He sneered. "I've had quite enough help. I don't need more, and I don't need you. I'm not one of your patients you can stick a bandage on and heal, Grace. I'm broken, really broken, and I refuse …" He stopped and slumped against the wall, as though all the fight flowed out of him. "Please just go, Grace. Please go. Go away and don't come back. I don't ever want to see you again."

"It might be best if you left now," Gary said softly.

Grace didn't want to leave. Everything in her shouted at her to stay, to make Levi see they could get through this, through any challenge, if they faced it together.

But it seemed Levi preferred to face them alone.

Tears spilled from her eyes and rained down her cheeks as Grace turned and ran out to her car. Until Levi realized he needed help, there wasn't anything she could do for him.

The truth of it broke her heart.

11

"Levi, would you at least stop long enough to listen?" Gary asked, rushing to keep up with Levi's long, furious strides as he walked across the end of a beet field to make sure the irrigation water had made it from one end to the other.

"I don't need to listen. You and Ma have done nothing but harp at me for weeks, Pop. I heard you the first fifty times."

"Obviously, you didn't!" Gary grabbed Levi's shoulders, forcing him to stop and face him.

Levi had never considered hitting his father, but at that moment, his hand curled into a fist, and he thought about how satisfying it would feel to punch him in the nose.

"You are on the fast track to destruction, son, and your mother and I can't watch you do this to yourself. You need help. Why won't you just admit it, accept it, and do what you need to do to move on with your life?"

"Because!" Levi jerked away from his dad and took a few more angry steps before the insistent man stopped him again.

"Because why, Levi? Because isn't a reason."

"It's enough of a reason. Please, Pop, just leave it be."

Gary sighed. "No. We've let you wallow in your misery for three weeks, Levi. You aren't sleeping. When you do, I know you're having terrible dreams. You jump at every loud noise, and you nearly took a chunk out of Tucker's hide yesterday when all he did was accidentally drop a bale of hay close to you. Worse than any of that, though, you've withdrawn from Grace, spurning her attempts to help you and pushing her out of your life. We all know how much you love her. She is the single best thing that has ever happened to you. One day you are going to wake up and regret losing her. Don't let it happen, son. There's still time to turn this thing around and get it headed in the right direction."

"What direction is that, Pop? The crazy house? Isn't that where they stick people like me who freak out at fireworks shows and have to be carried out of the crowd by strangers? How do you think I could possibly have a life with Grace when I'm terrified of what I might do to her in my sleep? What if we have kids, and I hurt one of them when I'm lost in one of my flashbacks? I couldn't live with myself if I ever hurt her. It's better to just let her go now, Pop. I can't ruin her life. Not when she's …" Levi heaved a soul-weary sigh. "Please, Pop, let it be."

"No. Either you make an appointment to go speak to the doctor Grace recommended, or your mother and I will do it for you. You aren't listening, Levi. Just because you've hit a rough patch doesn't mean that's the way things will always be. With the proper treatment, you can still live a full, happy life with the woman you love. You can deny it all you want, but you love Grace. You adore her. The happiest I've ever seen you—ever—is when you were with her. You need to be with Grace, and she needs to be with you. What will it take for you to see you don't have to give up on your dreams or your happiness?"

"You aren't going to change my mind, Pop. I'm broken beyond repair, and now that everyone knows it, I can't stuff that back in the box where I was doing a pretty good job of keeping it."

Levi started walking again. He'd only taken a few steps when his father jerked on his arm and spun him around. For the first time in his life, his father looked like he wanted to pummel some sense into him.

Caught off guard by the anger radiating from his father, Levi withdrew further into himself. The past three weeks had been the worst of his life. His mother hadn't stopped crying since the night Grace and Cindy had brought him home in what his father referred to as his trauma trance.

Levi had awakened that morning to find his father sitting by his bed, appearing haggard and old. He'd sat up and looked around his boyhood bedroom with no recollection of how he'd gotten there. The last thing he'd remembered was laughing with Grace and Cindy as the fireworks show had begun.

After questioning his father several times, he'd finally gotten him to explain about the girls bringing him home after two strangers helped load him in the car.

Levi's emotions had run the gamut from abject horror, because of what he might have done if Grace hadn't quickly removed him from the situation triggering him to think he was back in Vietnam, to unmitigated mortification that she'd seen him in such a state. According to what his father had shared, Grace had treated him like a patient, checking his pulse, making him comfortable. Knowing that she'd done that had infuriated him beyond the point of reason. He had ranted and raved for an hour, not making any more sense to himself than he did to his two bewildered parents.

Then Grace had shown up, and he'd all but tossed her out on her ear. And it was such a perfectly shaped, delicate ear.

Levi had known as soon as his father had told him what had happened that he had to end things with Grace. How had he let them go this far in the first place? He'd known all along he couldn't marry her. Not when he had no control of his dreams or the terrors that visited him most nights. He couldn't ask Grace to deal with the darkness that felt like it was about to consume him.

If he'd lost every last lick of sense and asked her to marry him, and she'd agreed, he might never be able to sleep again, worrying he'd hit her or something worse as one of his nightmares consumed him.

Grace had called twice and come out once, begging him to accept the help she offered, but he'd refused.

The more he was pushed to get help, the harder he resisted. It wasn't just pride. There was something simmering in him, something he couldn't describe or explain, that made him want to be mad and sullen. It gave him an excuse to lash out in anger.

Which was all the more reason he ought to listen to his parents and Grace and seek out a professional who might be able to help him through whatever was happening to him.

Regardless of what he should do, he continued to resist all offers of help.

"Levi, I love you more than life itself, but you are the only one who can make this better. It's your choice. Even if you remove Grace from the equation, you still need to find a way to heal for your own sake. Not for her. Not for your mother. Not for me or anyone else. You need to do it for you. To give yourself a chance at a future instead of letting what happened over there redefine who you are."

Levi thought of a few choice things he could say to his father. Before he could utter a word, the man turned and stormed off, leaving Levi alone in his misery.

Exactly where he thought he should be.

Miserable and alone.

He finished the morning irrigating and went to his house for lunch. Too tired and despondent to care about food, he threw off his clothes and took a cooling shower. Because he couldn't seem to keep his eyes open, he crawled into bed and immediately fell asleep.

Visions from the war he longed to forget taunted him, then Grace was there, mingling in the scenes flickering through his mind. He wanted to protect her. To keep her safe, but she kept drifting farther and farther beyond his reach.

"Grace," he yelled, reaching for her, then jolted awake, sitting upright in bed to find his father standing over him, worry grooving furrows across his brow.

"Call the doctor, Levi. What have you got to lose at this point?" His father handed him a slip of paper, then walked out of the house.

He recognized Grace's elegant script and held the paper to his nose, breathing in the slightest hint of her fragrance. He would forever associate the scent of pineapple with her.

One afternoon, as his mother had been flipping through a magazine last month, when the future still seemed hopeful instead of bleak, she'd shown him an article about how pineapples had been used by the colonists as a symbol of warmth and friendly welcome.

Levi had realized that was Grace. Friendly. Warm. Caring. Welcoming. Kind even when some—namely him—didn't deserve it.

He sat on the edge of the bed, staring at the name and number written on that piece of paper until his vision blurred.

He thought about Grace and how much joy, light, and love she'd brought into his life. He thought of his parents and how much worry and heartache he'd given them. He thought of his friends who'd gone off to war and returned home in caskets. He thought of the people who'd supported him and the ones who'd reviled him.

Memories of his childhood flowed into memories of the war, then ebbed into sweet memories of Grace.

He didn't want to spend his life mired in darkness. It wasn't who he was and definitely wasn't who he wanted to be. He could feel the shadows marring his soul grow more powerful by the day, and felt helpless to stop it, to change it.

His parents and Grace were right. He needed help. Desperately needed it.

When he finally glanced at the clock, he was shocked to see it was nearly six in the evening. He'd spent all afternoon lost in his thoughts.

Levi got dressed, made a sandwich, then went out and took care of his evening responsibilities on the farm. The next morning, after he'd completed his chores, he picked up the phone and called the number he'd memorized after staring at it so long the previous day. Levi answered several questions, and then the nurse made an appointment for him to come in that afternoon.

Before he did anything else, Levi went to tell his parents he'd made the call and to apologize for all he'd put them through.

All three of them were in tears by the time he finished speaking from his heart, confessing his pride, which had made him see the need for help as weakness, and sharing his fear that the darkness would continue growing until it consumed him. Finally, he returned to his house, showered, and changed, too nervous about the appointment to bother with lunch.

While he waited to leave for the appointment, he did something he knew he should have done months ago, spending time on his knees in prayer. When he left the house, it was with a glimmer of hope in his heart that maybe not all was lost.

He arrived half an hour early and made a point of avoiding the doctor's office where Grace worked. The last thing he needed right now was to run into her. He found the right office on a floor above Grace's, checked in with the receptionist, and quietly sat down to wait.

Levi kept his gaze glued to the floor until his name was called, then he followed a woman wearing a pretty summer dress into a spacious office splashed with light from multiple windows. The walls were a calming blue, the furniture nondescript but comfortable as Levi sank onto a leather chair.

"Mr. Gibson, I'm Dr. Becker. Let's talk about what I can do to help you."

Levi immediately liked the middle-aged man and spent the next hour answering questions and revealing more about his experiences in Vietnam than he'd shared with anyone.

When he left, with an appointment for two days later, Levi felt better than he had since the Fourth of July. To share some of what was bothering him with someone he felt wouldn't judge him had lifted a weight he hadn't even realized he was carrying.

It was after his third session, an hour spent with anger pouring out of him in a manner that freed and released it, that Levi got into his pickup to drive home and turned on the radio. As he left the hospital, he fiddled with the dial until he found the station Grace preferred and listened to Bill Withers sing "Lean on Me." The song was all about leaning on one another because everyone needed a hand from time to time.

Levi realized that was what his parents and especially Grace had been trying to get him to realize. He didn't need to carry this burden all alone. He could lean on them in his time of need without embarrassment or anger or fear. He could lean on them out of love.

Then Levi acknowledged in all the weeks of turmoil, he'd never once turned to the One who was always there for him to lean on, to carry his burdens, and renew his hope. Feeling convicted for his lack of faith, Levi opened his heart to God and sought forgiveness for his stubbornness and pride. He prayed for help to get him through his troubles and the strength to reach the other side.

Thoughts of Grace filled his mind, and he so badly wanted to go to her, but the timing wasn't right. Not yet.

But perhaps she wouldn't mind receiving a letter from him.

As soon as he got home, he wrote her a brief but heartfelt note and took it out to the mailbox, hoping it wouldn't take long to reach her. Then he found the card the World War II veteran had given him back in May, and he phoned James Jepson. In J.J., Levi had found both a friend and ally who completely understood what he had been through and the emotions he was dealing with now.

Over the next few weeks, Levi continued seeing Dr. Becker, continued renewing his faith, and continued missing Grace.

He'd written her half a dozen letters, and she'd replied to three of them, offering encouragement and support but not hinting of anything more.

For her sake, he should have let her go, but he couldn't. Not when he loved her to the very depths of his being. He'd apologized to her in his letters, but it wasn't enough. He needed to do it face-to-face.

On a hot afternoon near the end of August, he had an appointment to see both Dr. Becker and Dr. O'Brien. He finished with Dr. Becker and made his way to Dr. O'Brien's office, where he checked in with the receptionist and took a seat to wait. It wasn't long until a familiar voice called his name.

He stood, and his gaze collided with Grace's. Her beauty took his breath away for a moment. Almost two months had passed since his incident at the fireworks show, but it felt more like years. Just the sight of her filled his heart with an unexpected joyful feeling.

With a nod, he followed her to an exam room where she took his pulse and temperature with cool professionalism. When she leaned close to put the cuff around his arm to check his blood pressure, he couldn't help but breathe in her intoxicating scent.

Man, alive, but he'd missed her.

Everything in him shouted to take her in his arms, to apologize, to profess his love, and to promise her he'd never let anything come between them again. But the timing wasn't right. Not when she pressed her lips into a thin line and wrote notes in his medical chart as though he were nothing more than a patient.

Part of him did feel like a stranger to Grace. So much had changed in the last month. Thanks to Dr. Becker, Levi had only awakened twice with nightmares in the past three weeks. With the help of the techniques the doctor had taught him, he was able to calm down and go back to sleep.

With each session, Levi knew he made progress. At first, he did it for his loved ones, but now he did it for himself. For the sake of his soul and his own peace of mind. He needed to feel like he could help himself, but he'd learned the best help came not from a doctor or his own thoughts, but from God. When he accepted that, peace unlike anything he'd ever felt had flooded through him.

He wanted to share all that with Grace, but from the look on her face, the opportunity to do so may have passed entirely.

"Levi! So good to see you," Dr. O'Brien said as he hustled into the room. After giving him a quick checkup, testing his range of motion, and declaring him as fit as a fiddle, the doctor told him he didn't need to come back for six months.

This was great news for Levi, although he caught a look of despair flash across Grace's face as the doctor left the room.

Levi stood and pulled on his shirt, slowly fastening the snaps while keeping his gaze locked on her. She busied herself tidying the already clean room, then fussed with an imaginary speck of lint on her uniform. He tucked in his shirt, aware of her watching him from the corner of her eye.

When he was dressed, with his hat in his left hand, he took a step toward the door, then stopped. The electrical sparks between the two of them that popped around the room were almost something Levi could see. It made him hopeful that things weren't entirely over with Grace, at least not yet.

On a chance, he lifted her hand with his and kissed the backs of her fingers.

She jerked her hand away and glared at him, but he smiled at her. A smile of apology.

"I'm truly and deeply sorry, Grace, for acting like I did when you were only trying to do what was best. I was in a bad place, as you pointed out, and needed help. Dr. Becker is amazing, and I'm so very thankful you suggested I give him a call. I just wanted to let you know I'm doing much better, and a large part of that is thanks to you. I hope someday you can forgive me, Grace. If you ever want to be friends again, you know where to find me."

Before she could say a word, he tipped his head to her and left the room. Instead of worrying about what might happen, he decided to just leave it all in the Creator's capable hands.

Lighter in heart than he'd been for a long, long time, Levi drove home whistling along to the radio. The song that played, about seeing clearly after the rain had gone, was exactly how Levi felt. He'd been trapped in a horrible, stormy place that had left him mired in darkness. But the sun had finally broken through the clouds, and he could clearly see the light around him, within him, once again.

Saturday morning, Levi awakened with one thought on his mind.

Go to Grace.

Those three words played over and over until he nearly raced out to the pickup and sped into town. Only by sheer will did he resist the urge to go to her. As he pulled on his work clothes and then headed out to irrigate, a little voice continued whispering to his heart.

Go to Grace.

Two hours later, Levi rode his motorbike to his parents' home, arriving just before they sat down for breakfast. Of course, his mother insisted on him joining them and quickly fixed a plate for him. She took a seat, and the three of them bowed their heads while his father asked a blessing on their meal and the day before them.

It wasn't until his father was slathering fresh peach jelly over his second piece of toast that Levi spoke up, sharing what was on his mind.

"I woke up this morning with the thought that I need to go to Grace. While I was doing the irrigating, the voice just kept whispering 'Go to Grace.' Even now, it's there in the back of my mind, nudging me to go to Grace. What do you think I should do?"

His parents looked at each other, then at him. "Go to Grace!" they shouted in unison.

Levi dropped his fork, hopped up from the table, and ran out the door to the sound of their laughter floating out the open windows.

He sped home, showered and shaved, and dressed in a newer pair of jeans, a blue plaid shirt Grace had always favored, and was just tamping his feet into his boots when he heard gravel crunching outside as a car approached.

"Go to Grace," he whispered, and ran out the door.

12

"This is ridiculous. Just drive over there and talk to him." Cindy scowled at Grace as the two of them sat in front of a window with a table fan blowing over a bowl full of ice cubes in an effort to cool off.

Their apartment, being on the second floor, seemed to hold all the heat that came up from the first one. For a few months in the summer, it could be almost unbearable.

Only Grace was far less concerned about the heat and far more worried about her feelings for Levi.

After he'd told her with unmistakable clarity that he never wanted to see her again, she'd finally given up on reaching him. Of course, Stella had kept her updated on how he was doing, although Grace was convinced Levi and his dad knew nothing about the notes Stella mailed to her or the phone calls they exchanged when the men were out working.

Grace's prayers had been answered when she'd found out Levi had finally started seeing Dr. Becker. She knew from other patients at the hospital that the well-trained physician could help Levi get back on even footing and learn ways to cope with issues that might arise in the future.

It had been so hard for her to take a big step back from the man she loved when all she wanted to do was hold him, love him, and support him.

When he'd first pushed her away, she'd been confident he'd change his mind. Only he hadn't. She'd been angry, then hurt, followed by a yearning to bargain with him, to do whatever she could to get him the help he needed, even if it meant he'd permanently block her from his life.

Finally, she'd accepted that Levi had to come to terms with his problems and want to seek help all on his own. If there was still a chance for them to be together somewhere down the road, then it would all work out.

The moment she'd realized he was coming in for an appointment at Dr. O'Brien's office, Grace had made sure she was the attending nurse. She'd needed to see him, even if she kept her demeanor professional and reserved.

But then Levi had apologized. Sincerely. From his heart. When he'd kissed the backs of her fingers, her knees had weakened to the point she wasn't sure they'd continue holding her upright. He'd thanked her, then invited her to come out to the farm sometime.

She assumed he meant sometime far in the future, not mere days later, but it seemed to be all she could think about since he'd been at the doctor's office the other day.

Now, she and Cindy were spending their Friday evening trying not to roast as heat flowed into the apartment in miserable waves.

Grace took a cool shower and went to bed, hoping to distract herself with a new book she'd borrowed from one of the other nurses, but she couldn't keep her focus on it with her mind continually drifting to Levi.

She turned off her light and tried to sleep, but it came in fitful snatches with dreams of Levi. Only they weren't sad dreams, but more like glimpses of the future they might have had together. She could see sunsets, picnics, horseback rides, laughter, and babies with her hair and his eyes.

Finally, she fell into a restful sleep and awakened knowing what she needed to do.

After dressing and getting ready for the day, she pulled the gun case from beneath her bed where she'd been keeping it and took out the parchment from the pocket, reading the letter once again. When she finished, she tucked the letter back into the case, picked up the pistol, and closed her eyes.

"I open my heart to the joys, sorrows, dreams, and reality of love, to the hope that the man who'll love me truly, fiercely, faithfully, and tenderly for the rest of my life is Levi, and we'll spend a lifetime growing deeper in love each day," Grace whispered, then set the pistol back in the case. She stepped into the hallway and bumped into Cindy, who looked sleepy as she wrapped her in a hug. "Tell Levi I said hello."

Grace returned Cindy's hug after shifting the pistol case beneath her arm. "I will. I don't know what time I'll be back."

"It's fine. I'll do the laundry and then maybe go to the park. It has to be cooler there."

"I'll see you later, Cindy, and thank you for being such a good friend."

"Always. Now, go wrangle your fella or whatever it is you're supposed to do with your magic pistol."

Grace rushed out to her car and drove to Star, unaware of the humidity, other vehicles on the road, or the storm clouds gathering overhead. When she turned onto Gibson property, she felt a slight trepidation of what Levi might say when she showed up unexpectedly, but she cast aside her doubts and bravely headed directly toward his house. She didn't know why she felt he'd be there instead of out working in one of the fields. All she knew was that she needed to get to his house, to him.

She drove faster than she probably should have on the country road, but she felt such an urgency to reach Levi.

When his house came into view, she breathed a sigh of relief. She'd barely stopped outside when he yanked open the front door and took the porch steps in one giant leap.

Two more long strides and he was at the car, rushing around to open her door and pulling her into his arms.

No words were needed as he held her to him, murmuring in her ear how much he'd missed her, how sorry he was to have driven her away. Then he kissed her with a mixture of hunger and tenderness.

"What are you doing here?" he asked as he leaned back but kept both arms wrapped around her.

"I can't explain it, but I just had to come see you, Levi. I know this will sound crazy, but I read the letter that came with the pistol again, and then I just felt this need to be here, with you."

"It's not crazy, Miss American Pie." He brushed a lock of hair behind her ear and hugged her again like he never wanted to let her go. "I woke up with three words going over and over in my thoughts."

"What words?" she asked, pushing back from him just enough she could see his face.

"'Go to Grace.' Those words repeated nonstop as I irrigated and even while I sat down to eat breakfast with Ma and Pop. When I told them, they both shouted at me to go to you. I was just changing my clothes, and here you are, and I'm so glad." Levi released a long breath. "Grace, I was so awful to you. I'm sorry, so deeply and incredibly sorry. I pushed you away because I didn't want to hurt you, but I ended up doing that anyway. I promise, if you'll give me a second chance, I'll never, ever do that again. Is there any hope that you might forgive me? Perhaps consider the possibility of a future together?"

"Of course, I forgive you. I'm a big believer in second chances, you know." Grace grinned and pulled him closer for another kiss. Since she'd been the one to ask Levi for a first date, she supposed she might as well plunge ahead and share what was on her heart. "I love you, Levi Gibson, and I have from the first day we met. As for considering the possibility of a future together, I would love for it to come true. We can move at whatever speed is comfortable for you. I just … I don't know how to explain it, Levi, but the first time I held that pink pistol in my hand, I opened my heart to the possibility of love. This morning, when I closed my eyes and envisioned love, your face was the only thing I could see. I truly love you with all my heart."

Levi swung her around, then stepped back from her, holding her left hand in his right. "I have absolutely no right to ask this, Grace, but I love you with all my heart, and I have from the first day we met when you terrorized me with your thermometer, making me fearful of what you might actually do with it if I didn't open my mouth."

She grinned and lifted an eyebrow. "You stubborn types need to know when I mean business."

"Yes, we do." Levi brought her fingers to his mouth and kissed the backs of them, then continued. "It would be my greatest honor and privilege if you would agree to marry me, Grace. If you want to live here, that's grand, but if you prefer to move to Holiday, your dad mentioned some land for sale south of town where he thought potatoes might grow."

"We'll stay here, Levi, and raise our family to be the fifth generation of Gibsons on this land."

He smirked and waggled his eyebrows at her. "If you're talking about having my babies, might I assume that means you'll marry me?"

"Yes, yes, and yes!" Grace shouted.

Levi picked her up, swinging her around a second time before he let her slide down until their lips connected in a fiery kiss full of passion.

"Hey, you two. Save some of that for the honeymoon!" a deep male voice called from behind them.

Grace spun around and squealed, racing to throw her arms around her brother Jared as he walked toward them, holding Cindy's hand. After weeks of delays, he'd finally made it home in one piece.

"Nice to meet you," Jared said, holding out a hand to Levi once Grace turned loose of him.

"Welcome home," Levi said with a friendly smile.

Just then, thunder boomed overhead, and rain started to pour from the skies.

Jared grabbed Cindy's hand while Levi took Grace's, and the four of them raced inside the house to start making wedding plans.

"I don't think I've ever seen a more beautiful bride," Cindy gushed, adjusting Grace's veil as they readied in the basement of the church in Holiday for Grace and Levi's wedding.

The gown Grace wore, covered in rich Irish lace, had belonged to Grace's mother, and Jo-Ann's mother before her. The sweetheart neckline inset with lace that rose high on her neck and the lace sleeves that were puffed from shoulder to elbow and then tight to her wrist definitely had a Victorian look to them, which Grace loved.

Cindy, the maid of honor, and the three bridesmaids, wore lace-trimmed Gunne Sax dresses that had a years-gone-by vibe to them.

"Thank you for everything, my friend," Grace said, giving Cindy a tight hug, then stepping back before she wrinkled her dress or started to cry and smeared the makeup the two of them had so carefully applied.

"Of course, Grace. I'm just so happy for you and Levi and elated the two of you will stay in Star."

Grace gave her a sly grin. "You're mostly elated because Jared has moved to Boise and is rooming with one of Levi's cousins. It was such perfect timing that a mechanic job opened up when it did, and Levi's uncle let us know about it."

Cindy nodded, then fluffed the skirt of Grace's gown. "I think God's timing is always perfect."

"Indeed, it is." Grace smiled at her friend with love and then accepted the bouquet that Cindy held out to her. The burgundy and peach hues of the flowers in the bouquet were perfect for a fall wedding.

A knock sounded at the door and it swung open as Grace's father stepped inside, eyes bright with emotion.

"I'll go see if everyone is ready," Cindy said, rushing out of the room.

"Oh, Gracie, girl, aren't you a picture!" her dad said as he strode across the room and gave her an enveloping hug. "How can you be all grown up and ready to marry that fine young man of yours when I still want to think of you as my little sidekick, tagging along after me on adventures?"

"I'll always be your little girl, Daddy, but I love Levi with all my heart."

Mike Marshall patted her hand. "I know you do, and he feels the same about you, or I never would have given that boy permission to marry you."

Grace couldn't hide her surprise. "When did he ask you?"

"Back in June, when he came for Delia's wedding. I asked him what his intentions were, and he was honest with me about being uncertain at the moment. But he did ask your mother and me if we'd give him our blessing to marry you. After meeting him and seeing the two of you together, it was as plain as day you two were, and are, in love."

"I am, Daddy. I just can't picture a day in my future without Levi in it."

Her father smiled and kissed her cheek. "That means he's the one you are meant to spend your life with, sweetheart." He took a step back. "For a moment, she thought the mist in his eyes might end up with them both in tears. She'd never seen her father cry and didn't want today to be the day she had that memory. She wanted her wedding day to be one full of joy.

"Before you start blubbering all over me," she joked, hoping to lighten the mood, "we should probably head upstairs."

"Cindy will let us know when it's time," he said, winking at her, his good humor restored. "Did you get all the traditional trappings a bride is supposed to have?"

Grace nodded. "Levi's mother gave me these earrings for something old." She pointed to her ears.

Stella had tapped on the door an hour ago and held out a small blue velvet box. Inside were a delicate pair of pearl earrings.

"These belonged to Gary's mother, and she gave them to me on my wedding day. If you have a son, pass them on to his bride. We're so, so pleased, Grace, to be getting you for a daughter, darling." Stella had kissed her cheek and hurried from the room before they both dissolved in tears.

"What else do you have?" Mike asked, looking her over from head to toe.

"My something new is a silly thing, I suppose, but it means a lot to me." Grace held up her bouquet and pointed to a bullseye pin she'd fastened to ribbons where no one but she could see it. "Cindy got this to remind me that when our aim is true, anything is possible. It's also because the first time I went shooting with Levi, he teased me about making a lucky shot, but the luckiest thing that happened to me was meeting him. I like to think God had plans for us all along."

"I'd say you both are blessed, Gracie. Not everyone finds what you and Levi have with each other." Her father squeezed her hand that wasn't holding the bouquet. "What else do you have?"

"Gary gave me a penny that I have in my shoe for something borrowed, and something blue is a handkerchief that belonged to Grandma. It has little blue flowers embroidered in the corner. Mom said she carried it on her wedding day. Since you seem to still like each other, at least a little," Grace teased, thinking about how much in love her parents remained, even after four kids and all the years that had passed, "it seemed like the perfect thing to be my something blue."

"That's great, sweetheart. Your mom and I are—"

"It's time," Cindy said, poking her head into the room with a broad smile. "Levi looks like he's ready to bolt."

"Don't say that to her," Mike warned, then chuckled as Cindy darted out of the doorway. Grace could hear the church organ playing, and the noise overhead suddenly stilled.

"If you're having doubts, I can sneak you out the back door," her father offered, looking serious, although she could hear the mirth in his voice.

"Not a single doubt, Daddy. I can't wait to become Grace Gibson."

He helped her settle the veil over her face, and then they made their way upstairs. The moment she stepped into the aisle strewn with burgundy and peach rose petals, it was as if all the friends and family there melted away until the only person she could see was Levi.

The love he held for her in his heart shone in his eyes as he smiled at her and took her hand when she and her father reached him. Grace swallowed a giggle when her father gave Levi a menacing scowl before taking a seat in the front row next to her mother.

The ceremony was brief but poignant, and when they exchanged the vows they'd written, Grace heard more than one person sniffling in the crowd. When the pastor gave them permission to kiss, Grace had no idea what to expect. Would Levi be too shy to give her a kiss worthy of a new bride, or would he go overboard and give her one that made her blush?

Slowly, he raised her veil, cupped her cheek and then her chin, and delivered a kiss that was both tender and reverent but with just enough promise of things to come that several of Grace's cousins sighed at the romantic sight.

Since the weather had not yet turned cold and the day arrived without a hint of rain, they'd opted to hold their reception outdoors. White tablecloths fluttered in the gentle autumn breeze, while sunshine glimmered through the leaves of the trees that had only begun to turn from green to the rich shades of gold, crimson, and vermillion.

Her brothers had constructed a temporary dance floor. For the first song as husband and wife, Grace had requested "The First Time Ever I Saw Your Face." As she and Levi swayed to the song, she saw Stella and her mother both dabbing at their tears.

Grace shifted her attention back to her husband. She could hardly believe it. She was married to the man of her dreams. All she'd had to do was open her heart to love and pray that she'd know him when she met him.

And she had.

"I love you so much, Miss American Pie," Levi whispered in her ear as they danced. "You are so beautiful and dear to my heart. I'm so grateful you agreed to spend the rest of your life with me. I vow to do my best to show you every day how precious you are to me."

Grace smiled and leaned back slightly in his arms to better see his face. "Do you have any idea how much I treasure you, Levi, and your love?"

"I'm starting to get an idea," he said with a grin.

Later, when they were ready to leave for their honeymoon in Seattle, Grace returned to the basement room with Cindy to change out of her wedding gown and into a new navy blue traveling suit with a burgundy and navy paisley blouse that was a gift from Cindy and her mom.

She picked up her purse to leave, then stopped and spun around. "I almost forgot to write the note!"

She took out the pink pistol case she'd brought back to Holiday, carefully removed the parchment letter, and scanned the notes previous brides who'd been in possession of the revolver had written. Some made her laugh, and a few grabbed onto her heart. Without overthinking what to write, she picked up a pen and added her own message to the paper.

Grace Marshall wed Levi Gibson amid autumn's splendor on October 15, 1972. He called me a lucky shot, but what I really am is lucky in love to marry the man I love with all my heart and soul.

Grace blew on the ink so it would dry quickly, tucked the note back into the case, and gave the case to her best friend. "You'll make sure it gets mailed?"

"I will do that first thing tomorrow," Cindy promised, then gave Grace a one-armed hug. "Have the best time with Levi, Grace. Both of you deserve happiness without measure."

Grace smiled as they hurried back upstairs. "I intend to do everything I can to make our home a peaceful, joyful place full of warmth and love."

"You've already done that to my heart," Levi said, slipping behind her and kissing the spot beneath her ear that made delightful sensations slide along her spine. "Are you ready to walk into the future—our future—together?"

"No," Grace said, grinning at him as she laced their fingers together and tugged him toward the door. "With you, I'd much rather run!"

Outside, their guests cheered, pelting them with rice and rose petals. Grace heard Levi's laughter as he attempted to shield her from the worst of it as they dashed to her car. After he helped her inside, he bent down and kissed her softly.

"I love you, Grace Gibson, and I have a feeling today is only the beginning of what will be years ahead full of happiness, laughter, and so much love."

She placed her hand on his cheek. "Then may it be so, Levi. May it always be so."

Continue reading for an excerpt from the next Pink Pistol Sisterhood sweet romance,
Aiming for His Heart.
Also, enjoy an excerpt from *Lake Bride*, a sweet romance set in the town of Holiday!

Pineapple Cookies

I inherited a 1961 Betty Crocker cookbook from my grandma. When I started working on this story, it was one of the first things I plopped onto my desk next to my computer, so I could look up food Grace would have been making or enjoying. My hubby, Captain Cavedweller, loves all things pineapple, so I had to try the recipe for pineapple cookies. The first attempt lacked enough pineapple flavor, but this updated version was a hit with CC. So, I had Grace bake them for Levi. I hope you enjoy these flavorful cookies if you give them a try!

Pineapple Cookies

INGREDIENTS

1 cup crushed pineapple
½ cup butter
1 cup brown sugar, packed
1 egg
1 teaspoon vanilla extract
½ teaspoon lemon juice
2 cups all-purpose flour
1 ½ teaspoons baking powder
¼ teaspoon baking soda
½ teaspoon salt
1 12-ounce bag white chocolate chips
½ cup chopped macadamia nuts (optional)
1 ½ cups powdered sugar
Candied Pineapple pieces (optional)

DIRECTIONS

Preheat oven to 325 degrees. Line a baking sheet with parchment and lightly coat with non-stick cooking spray.

Drain pineapple (leave a little juice in the pineapple, don't drain it dry) reserving 1/3 cup of the juice for the frosting.

In a mixing bowl, cream together butter and brown sugar until light and fluffy. Beat in egg, pineapple, and vanilla.

In another bowl combine flour, baking powder, baking soda, and salt and stir or whisk until thoroughly mixed. Add dry ingredients to the creamed ingredients. Stir in chips and nuts.

Use a tablespoon (or cookie scoop) to drop cookie dough onto the baking sheet about 2 inches apart. The cookies will spread.

Bake for 17 minutes, or until cookies are barely starting to brown.

Transfer cookies to wire racks to cool.

Mix powdered sugar and reserved pineapple juice in a small bowl. Glaze the cookies, top with tiny pieces of candied pineapple, if desired, and enjoy!

Yield: about 24 cookies

Thank You

Thank you for reading *Lucky Shot*. Now that you've finished, will you please consider writing a review? It means so much when a reader leaves a review, and I'm truly so grateful.

Also, please subscribe to my newsletter. You'll receive a free book or two, and what I call *The Welcome Letters* with exclusive content and some fun stuff! My newsletters are sent when I have new releases, sales, or news of freebies to share. Each month, you can enter a contest, get a new recipe to try, and discover details about upcoming events. Don't wait. Sign up today!

If newsletters aren't your thing, please follow me on *BookBub*. You'll receive notifications on pre-orders, new releases, and sale books!

If you enjoyed reading about the town of Holiday and the characters there, be sure to read **Holiday Hope.** This sweet historical romance is where the town really begins. Also, be sure to read **Henley** if you'd like to know more about Doctor Evan and Henley Holt.

Keep reading for an excerpt from the next Pink Pistol Sisterhood story, *Aiming for His Heart*, and a peek at *Lake Bride*, a contemporary sweet romance set in the town of Holiday.

Author's Note

I wasn't expecting to write this story, since I wrote *Love on Target* early in the Pink Pistol Sisterhood series, but when the opportunity arose, a little voice whispered in my thoughts saying, "Write this story." I'm so glad I did!

Why did I choose the Boise and Star area for the setting? It's because I grew up in the Treasure Valley. Although I was just a baby when *Lucky Shot* takes place, so many memories from my childhood flooded over me when I began writing the story. Gosh, I had a great time, skipping along memory lane while incorporating those details into Levi and Grace's journey to their happily ever after.

I'll start with the orange and white Chevy pickup Levi purchased. It just so happens my dad purchased the same pickup in 1972. You can see a photo of Captain Cavedweller and Dad riding in it on my blog. My dad had a gun rack in the pickup that I hung onto when I was really little as I stood next to him. We had so many fun adventures in that pickup (and did a lot of farm work with it too). It will always remind me of my childhood and summers spent out in the sunshine with Dad.

My second brother was the one in our family who was goofy over cars, and I remember him talking about the Firebird Raceway in Eagle. It was the inspiration for the raceway where Levi, Grace, and Cindy watched the drag races before the disastrous fireworks show.

My dad and brother also liked their motorcycles. As far back as my memory goes, they rode them to irrigate until Dad got a 4-wheeler in the 1980s. Dad had a scabbard on the side of his motorbike to hold his shovel, and he had an assortment of tools in case he needed them. I even had my own motorbike from the time I was eleven so I could help on the farm.

Karcher Mall was a very real place that I loved to visit. As a little girl, I thought it was so "fancy" with red carpeted halls and department stores unlike anything we had in our small town. There really was a big polar bear with a seal in a glassed-in case in the mall that was both scary and fascinating to look at! Karcher Mall was the very first mall in Idaho, opening in 1965, and remained the largest until Boise Towne Square opened in 1988.

Another real place included in the story is the Egyptian Theatre in Boise. It has been around since the 1920s, has the most fascinating style, and has been a landmark for decades.

My dad recently mentioned a store in Star called Jackson's that carried, according to him, "a little bit of everything." It was fun to work that into the story.

My sister had several health problems and one of the doctors she saw was in Boise. His name was Dr. O'Brien. I thought he was awesome, probably because I always got candy from him when my sister had an appointment, and decided to use him as inspiration for one of the doctors in the office where Grace works.

In the story, when Levi is hustling to close the shop door, that idea came from memories of Dad (or my brother) running to close the big shop doors if a storm was brewing because if the wind caught them, they were toast.

I have seen photos of the wagon wheel furniture my parents once had. In fact, when they built their new house (where I was raised) they kept the wagon wheel chandelier. It hung in our family room and roughhousing children were known to knock the little metal tops off the glass lamp chimneys from time to time.

I'm so grateful I had my grandma's old 1961 Betty Crocker cookbook. It gave me so many ideas for the day-to-day things my characters would eat as well as recipes for special treats. I also looked to my 1970 Betty Crocker cookbook for kids for ideas. I loved that cookbook when I was first learning my way around the kitchen. I think it was a leftover relic from some of my older cousins, and several of the pages were missing, but the colorful images and illustrations made it such a fun thing to look through when I was young.

While I'm on the subject of food, I was a happy kid when Mom bought Carnation Breakfast Bars. They originally came out in 1975, so I fudged the timelines just a bit, but I so wanted to include them in this story. They were chocolate chip with chocolate coating, and I thought I was getting to eat candy for breakfast! I loved them, especially for an after-school snack! There is nothing out there today that compares to the taste of those original breakfast bars.

I also loved the assortment of gum and candy my dad often plied me with when we were off on an adventure (interpret as irrigating). We always had

Life Savers (Butter Rum was a favorite flavor) and Big Hunk candy bars as well as Necco Wafers, Bit-O-Honey, and little boxes of Lemonheads. I was a fan of Fruit Stripe gum too. Of course, almost every trip Dad and I made to town included getting a bottle of icy cold pop from a vending machine. Those real glass bottles held more Coca-Cola than I could drink, so I'd drink what I wanted (which was usually a few sips), then Dad would finish the rest.

I included the mention of cocktail peanuts and buttermints at Delia's wedding because it seemed to me every wedding we attended back in those days had bowls of peanuts and those melt-in-your-mouth pastel mints.

If you lived through the 1960s or 1970s, you'll remember Pyrex bowls with a variety of patterns on the side, as well as the popularity of Tupperware. I even remember my mom hosting a Tupperware party, where you learned the proper way to make the lids "burp" as you sealed them. I also remember my mom having a big cake plate with a dome. I think it was in that funky poppy red color popular in the 1970s.

The mention of Red Steer and the Ham'oneer is directly from my childhood. We had a Red Steer in a nearby town (and there were locations in the Boise area too). It's the town where Dad often had to go for parts in the summer, and we would sometimes swing by and get an ice cream cone or milkshake. When I got older, I remember ordering their famous Ham'oneer (that name was at one time trademarked). The hamburger was delicious on its own, but they added this thick, almost cottage-style bacon that elevated it to a whole new level of tastiness. Captain Cavedweller and I were both sad when all the Red Steers closed.

I had the best time looking through fashions from 1972. Mostly because they brought to mind clothes I remember seeing in Mom's closet. There was even a pair of slingback sandals similar to those worn by Grace in the story. I do believe those sandals met a sad and untimely death on the banks of the river in our small town when my oldest brother decided to ride his horse in the annual Suicide Race. Mom got so nervous, she clenched her legs and dug her feet into the banks so hard, it broke the heel off one of her favorite pairs of shoes! It made me feel close to Mom again to see dresses similar to those she had worn. I even found one advertisement for the outfit she wore to my grandparents' fiftieth wedding anniversary.

The dress Grace wore to Delia's wedding is inspired by a beautiful gown like it that my mom made for my sister. I thought the blue velvet burnout roses were so pretty.

When I started thinking about the music that would have been playing on the radio and record players back then, I had no idea so many songs that are still popular today came out in 1972! Although I shared several of them in the story, there's a great list my friend Cheryl shared with me. (Thanks, Cheryl! If you haven't yet, be sure to read her Pink Pistol story, *Love Under Fire*!) So many of the songs are familiar to me from listening to my mom sing along to them on the radio.

If you're wondering why I made Levi a recently returned soldier from Vietnam, I did it partly because I could just so clearly picture him as a wounded and struggling veteran. I also wanted to share a little about the war because it was such a big part of that time in our history. My deepest, most sincere thanks to anyone who is a veteran or is currently serving. Your service and sacrifices are appreciated more than you can know.

Check out the assortment of visuals that helped inspire tidbits in the story on my Pinterest board.

You can read more about the modern Gibson family in *Savoring Christmas*.

Special thanks to Katrina, Allison, Alice, Linda, and my Hopeless Romantic readers who make my books so much better than they'd be without their help. I appreciate you all so much.

Until we meet again between the covers of a book, wishing you joy in your heart and love in your home.

Shanna

Excerpt Copyright Information
from
Aiming for His Heart
(Pink Pistol Sisterhood Series)
by Julie Benson
Copyright © 2023 Julie Benson

She's all work and no play.
He aims to show her there's more to life.

Childhood disappointments and a bitter divorce taught Jade Buchanan that trusting her heart to a man leads to disaster. When she returns to Oklahoma to settle her aunt's estate, Jade discovers the cowboy hired to renovate the house is none other than Dalton Kelley, her first love. She's not worried, though. She has a solid plan—supervise the renovation like the adult she is, sell the property, and return to New York City with money to start a design company with her best friend. Simple. Until she starts working with Dalton and feelings she thought long dead bubble to the surface, raising havoc with her carefully laid plans.

Needing money thanks to cattle rustlers, Dalton hires on to renovate Jade's recently inherited house. Working for his teenage sweetheart will be awkward, but he can handle it in the short term. He'll collect his money, say goodbye to Jade, and find a woman without big city dreams to settle down with on his Done Roamin' Ranch. But the job brings trouble he hadn't counted on, and the more time he and Jade spend together, the less he can picture any other woman by his side.

For this city girl and small-town cowboy, will working together drive them crazy or into each other's arms?

Keep reading for an excerpt from the story!

Excerpt from Aiming for His Heart

by Julie Benson

Prologue

Sitting at her desk staring out the window at the gray January sky, love flowed through Rose Haddock as she thought of Josie, the daughter of her heart. Rose's fingers traced the delicate pink mother-of-pearl handled pistol nestled on a green velvet bed in its simple mahogany case. Even before she'd discovered the worn note inside the case's pocket, she'd been drawn to the pistol when she'd spotted it at the Bonner estate sale.

Rose believed people and objects often came into someone's life to teach a lesson or deliver a message. Since discovering the pistol, she'd known she was meant to continue its legacy with her sister Lily's only child and spitting image, Josie.

When she'd lost her sister, her promise to help raise Lily's then ten-year-old daughter had kept Rose going.

Lily, I'm worried about our girl. Since her divorce, she's closed herself off from love, and she's killing a part of herself.

Rose rubbed her hand against her breastbone, trying to ease the tightness and ache there. After digging antacids from her middle desk drawer and taking two, she waited for the pain to subside. Having felt this way too often lately, she added calling Dr. Sackrison to her to-do list. That done, Rose's thoughts returned to the pistol and Josie.

The pistol had been created to encourage women to open their hearts to love. The problem was her ever-practical and logical niece would consider the pistol and its legend a fanciful, but fictional—and futile—tale. But if Rose talked to Josie in person, explained her concerns and why Josie needed love in her life, maybe her niece would understand.

Unfortunately, Josie's visits had grown few and far between in the last years. Last week when Rose had asked her to visit, the conversation had gone predictably. Work was crazy. Maybe in a couple months she could visit, but something told Rose she couldn't wait for her niece. What if instead of asking Josie to come to Oklahoma, Rose went to New York City? Surely if she visited, Josie would make time for her.

Dismissing her nagging chest discomfort, what she'd say to her niece tumbled through her head. How would she ever remember it all? Needing to organize her thoughts, she retrieved stationery and a pen. *Don't just write notes. Write Josie a letter.* Always one to listen to her inner voice, especially when it spoke to her this emphatically, Rose started her letter.

My dearest Josie,

First, stop wrinkling your nose and sighing at my addressing this letter to Josie rather than Jade. While you may go by your middle name now, to me you'll always be my little Josie.

When I saw a beautiful, pink-handled pistol a month ago, it called to me. After buying the revolver, I discovered a letter inside the case. When I read it, I knew this beautiful piece was meant to be with you. Now reach into the case's pocket and read the note resting there.

Rose chuckled, imagining Josie reading that sentence. Her stubborn niece wouldn't put this note aside yet. She'd want to finish what she started before turning to the other note.

Josie, I know you're thinking you'll read the other note after you finish mine, but do as I say. Read the other one right now, young lady.

Now that you've read the other note, don't wrinkle your nose again, Josephine. I know true love isn't the answer to all problems. But I'm worried about you, and it's time I say so. In voicing my concerns, I believe I'm doing what your mom would have if she were alive.

The divorce has changed you. In some ways for the better, but in many for the worse. You always possessed an open, loving heart, and saw the best in people. You believed you could do anything you set your mind to. But since your divorce, I've seen a change in your spirit. Now I see a woman who's so afraid of making a mistake, she overthinks every decision. She fears being hurt, so she no longer trusts her judgment about people. I know you, and you're thinking you missed signs with Eric. Maybe you did, or maybe he was good at hiding what he didn't want you to see.

As you discovered, loving someone can bring us pain so dark we think there's no escape. When I lost your mother, I foolishly believed not ever having her in my life would've been better than dealing with my grief. But without her, I'd have missed years of love, memories, and what she taught me. I also never would've received my life's greatest gift—you.

Living shut off from the world may save you from pain, but it will rob you of joy, and that's not being truly alive. You can't give up on love. I believe love, even if it doesn't last, is never wasted. What love we create lives on long after we're gone, working magic in the world.

As the note says, accept the gift...or not. I'm hoping you choose hope and love.

Chapter One

"I was surprised when your name was on Raelynn's recommended contractor list. Did you get tired of ranch life and raising cattle?" Josie asked.

"Are you kidding? Not in this lifetime," Dalton Kelley said, filling his voice with what he hoped passed for a lighthearted tone. "But with droughts, natural disasters, and uncertain prices, ranching's unpredictable."

Or cattle rustlers could steal nearly half a herd throwing a body into financial chaos. This job would tide Dalton over and keep him from missing another mortgage payment until he received the insurance money. "Most ranchers take a second job now and again to keep a healthy emergency fund for rough patches."

Dalton glanced at his computer monitor. Though Josie had tried to tame her red hair into a frumpy bun, strands had escaped, forming a halo of fire around her face. Delicate high cheekbones accentuated her wide green eyes. Those eyes could capture a man and draw him in even before he realized she'd lassoed him. Dalton released his breath in a long, slow, controlled exhale.

How odd that holding on to the Done Roamin' Ranch that had been in his family for generations rested on convincing a woman he'd dated as a teenager, Josie Buchanan, to hire him.

From age ten until she'd left for college, Josie had spent every summer, a week at Christmas, and every spring break with her Aunt Rose. The last time he saw Josie, they'd sat by the creek on his ranch. He'd joked about how she should attend Oklahoma State instead of going to school in New York. Only he hadn't been joking.

"With all your ranch responsibilities, do you have time to devote to this renovation?" she asked, bringing his thoughts back to the present.

"Absolutely." It would take time management and sticking to a schedule, but he could do it. Waking early and staying up late to see to the chores might run him ragged, but he'd survive on two hours' sleep if that's what it took.

"Good, because despite our past association and all you did for my aunt and uncle over the years, if you aren't putting my job first, I'll find someone who will."

Past association? Was that how she saw him? He thought they'd been more. Each other's first kiss for sure, and she'd been his first love.

"I thought the world of Rose and George."

When his folks had retired to Florida, the couple had become his adopted local parents, inviting him for Sunday dinner and making sure he wasn't alone on holidays. He smiled, thinking of fishing with George. And Rose. Whenever he'd gone to mow the lawn, shovel snow, or see to whatever needed doing, she'd had brownies waiting and had insisted they chat. Dalton smiled again. Invariably those talks had always turned into her talking about Josie and grilling him about why he hadn't settled down. "I think of George whenever I use the fishing rod he gave me, and I'll never have a brownie again without thinking of Rose. Nobody's compares with hers."

"Do a good job, and I might share her secret recipe with you."

"Now that's incentive."

The irony of their situation hit him. The house Josie inherited had belonged to her family since 1911, but she couldn't sell the priceless gift fast enough. How could she do that when she'd spent much of her childhood there? He couldn't understand her not feeling a connection to the land and ancestors who'd shaped her.

He was the opposite because he couldn't imagine living anywhere but his family's land. Hopefully he'd raise children there one day should he find a woman who loved him enough to live with the financial uncertainty of ranch life.

Josie cleared her throat, pulling his attention back to her. "Once we deal with these final details, I'll send the contract for you to sign."

"I'm grateful for the job, Josie."

When her posture stiffened, her face scrunched up, and her eyebrows formed a V above her nose, he realized his mistake.

"I go by my middle name, Jade, now."

Rose had never said why Josie had started using her middle name, other than she felt it better suited her career and the image she wanted to portray. But what the heck did that mean?

"Sorry about that, but having known you for years as Josie, it'll take time to get used to calling you Jade."

"I'm sure you'll find it easier than you think. Now back to the project. I want to emphasize how important my timeline is. I absolutely—" Her phone pinged, indicating she'd received a text. Without saying anything to him, she grabbed her phone, read the message, and typed a reply.

After finishing, she said, "Sorry about that, but back to our conversation. With the information you gave me about the house, I feel my timeline is on target. What I need from you is reassurance you can finish in the allotted time."

Knowing she could see and hear him, Dalton resisted the urge to laugh and say didn't she know there were no guarantees in house renovations or life? "That's the plan, but—"

"Good," she said, cutting him off. "I can't be absent from the office longer than a month."

"You're taking a leave from work?" He'd assumed she'd oversee the project from New York and they'd connect either like this, via texts, or on phone calls.

She chuckled. "Certainly not. I'll be working remotely, but with finishing the fall catalog and photo shoots for a new marketing campaign, I don't dare stay away longer."

He nodded, not sure what she expected. Yeah, he got it. She was a big wig the company couldn't live without. But how crucial could things be in fashion?

"Just remember, as George used to say, there are only two guarantees in life—death and taxes," Dalton joked. "Unexpected issues come up with turn-of-the-century houses when walls start coming down."

A knock sounded on Jade's door, followed by a voice apologizing for the interruption and saying her signature was required. Jade muted their call. As she saw to the paperwork, Dalton saw visions of what working with her would be like. He'd twiddle his thumbs while she dealt with other business, but he'd be expected to hop to when she needed him. Yup, her time mattered more than his. Had she become an everything-was-an-emergency-to-be-handled-in-five-minutes person that believed the world revolved around her?

When her attention returned to him, Dalton said, "Do you want to call me back? Obviously, you're busy, and I have other things I could see to."

"I'll let calls go to voicemail until we finish." She set her phone aside where he couldn't see it. "Though I've never owned a house, researching renovating older ones on the internet made it clear unexpected issues can arise."

If she'd never owned a home, she had a landlord to see to problems. Heck, she probably hadn't ever replaced a light bulb much less been involved with serious renovations.

"Everyone thinks they've accounted for surprises, but a simple thing like a contractor's other jobs can mess up the schedule."

"If that happens, I'll hire someone who makes my job a priority."

Had she forgotten Loksi lacked a Walmart, McDonalds, or more than one plumber and electrician? Looked like reality would come hard and fast once she arrived. "That's your choice. I'll do everything I can to keep us on track. Sometimes materials are on backorder or shipping gets delayed by weather in the winter."

"That'll be my problem since I'll be doing the ordering to keep watch on costs."

More power to her, but he'd best warn Jerry at Everything for the House to double up on vitamins. From his interactions with Jade so far, working with her would be an exercise in patience.

"The last issue we need to discuss is your payment schedule," she said.

"What's to discuss?" He wiped his sweaty palms on his jeans. He needed the first half of his fee now. "Paying half at the start and the remainder at completion is standard."

"I've found with vendors that breaking payment into more installments associated with hitting targets ensures we remain on schedule. I suggest four payments associated with completing certain objectives."

No way. "That won't work for me."

"Should I find someone else?"

Dalton kept his breathing even and his features blank. He sure hoped he was a better poker player than Jade. "If you want to start over talking to contractors, that's up to you, but don't count on starting next week since Billy Bishop may have lined up another job."

He stared straight ahead, waiting, as he watched the gears turn in her mind. She hated backing down, but he'd bet she'd detest more her precious timeline getting off track before she ever started.

"What if we split the difference?" she asked.

"Deal."

"I think we're done, unless you have questions."

Having helped his father over the years with smaller renovations such as enlarging their kitchen, he knew what to expect with this job. "I'll see you Monday."

"I have a catalog photo shoot I can't miss, so I'll see you Tuesday morning at eight."

Something told Dalton he'd best rest up and increase his vitamins because working with Jade would test more than his patience.

Order your copy of
Aiming for His Heart
today!

**A solemn soldier.
A woman full of sunshine.
And the lake where they fall in love.**

Twenty-one steps. The past two years of Bridger Holt's life have centered on the twenty-one steps he repeatedly walks back and forth as one of the sentinels guarding the Tomb of the Unknown Soldier. Now that his duty is coming to an end, Bridger has no idea what to do with the rest of his life. Guilt from his past and trepidation about his unknown future drive him to the mountain cabin he inherited from his beloved uncle to gain clarity and direction. The quirky residents in the nearby town of Holiday, the assortment of wildlife that adopts him, and the woman who shines a light into his tattered soul might be what Bridger needs to find the redemption he seeks.

Outgoing, upbeat Shayla Reeves spreads sunshine wherever she goes. Holiday has become her home, and she enjoys spending time in the mountains around town. She adores the patients in the dementia facility where she works as a nurse. But something is missing from her mostly joyful world. When she mistakenly camps on private land owned by the mysterious and brooding Bridger Holt, she realizes what her life is lacking isn't adventure but love.

Will two opposite personalities overcome their challenges and figure out a way to build a future together?

Find out in this sweet love story full of hope, small-town humor, and the wonder of falling in love.

Lake Bride Excerpt

Snuggled into her sleeping bag, Shayla Reeves was in no hurry to get up and start the day. After all, today was her last day off. Tomorrow, it was back to the routine of providing nursing care at Golden Skies Retirement Village in Holiday, Oregon.

Shayla liked that she worked on a rotating schedule of four days on and four days off. The four days on could be brutal or fun, depending on what was going on with the residents at the retirement facility. Shayla spent the majority of her time working in the dementia wing. It broke her heart when the loved ones of her patients came in and left in tears because they were no longer recognized.

There were good things about her job, though. She liked being able to help patients who truly needed someone to be patient and kind with them as they navigated the murky waters of their once clear minds. Shayla had her favorite patients, and being able to make them smile made her days seem worthwhile.

Since the weather had been warm and gorgeous, Shayla had decided to spend her days off camping. She loved being outdoors and craved the fresh air and sunshine when she was working a long shift stuck inside.

Part of the reason she took her patients on walks outside each day was that she thought sunshine and breathing in the mountain air were helpful to their well-being. But another reason she liked to take them on those daily walks was her own need to be outside where she could feel the warmth of the sun on her shoulders or cheeks and where the fresh air could fill her lungs with the faint hint of pine that always seemed to linger on the breeze.

Shayla hadn't grown up in Holiday, but it had been home to her since she graduated from nursing school eight years ago. She'd taken a job at the hospital, working in a variety of positions including the emergency room.

When her friend Fynlee Ford had mentioned the new wing opening at Golden Skies, Shayla had practically jumped up and down in excitement at the opportunity to work there.

Although her friends referred to the facility as HPH, or the Hokey Pokey Hotel, Shayla enjoyed her job and the people she worked with there. Some of the residents, like colorful Matilda Dale and her sidekicks Ruth and Rand Milton, kept things from ever being dull.

Shayla rolled onto her back and smiled as she thought about Matilda and Ruth employing their matchmaking efforts to set her up with the cute doctor who'd joined the staff six months ago. Doctor Zach Huxley was in his early thirties, great with the patients, and pining after the woman he'd been dating in Montana before he moved to Holiday.

Only Matilda and Ruth seemed to be convinced if they shoved Shayla and Zach together, they'd fall madly in love. Shayla considered Zach a friend, but nothing more. They'd made the mistake of going out to dinner once, at Matilda's insistence, and the self-proclaimed matchmaker became twice as determined they belonged together. If Shayla had any brothers, she was sure her feelings for Zach would have easily fit in that category. She knew he had no romantic feelings for her either. Not when he constantly brought up Mindi from Montana. Shayla and Zach were coworkers and friends, but that was it. All it would ever be.

Before Zach, Matilda and Ruth had tried to connect her with Doctor Dawson, but he'd resigned quite suddenly when he married a pharmaceutical representative and moved to Portland right before Thanksgiving.

Shayla knew she wasn't the only one on the receiving end of Matilda and Ruth's efforts. It seemed if anyone in their sphere of contacts happened to be single, the two meddling old women began hatching happily-ever-after schemes.

Most of the time, it was entertaining to watch, as long as it didn't involve Shayla directly.

With a sigh, Shayla opened her eyes, ready to begin her day. At least the weather had been mild. She'd thought about sleeping with the tent flap open last night just to catch more of the breeze, but she hadn't wanted to awaken with a raccoon or goodness knew what else curled up against her side.

Shayla lifted her arms from the sleeping bag and stretched them over her head. The temperature hadn't dropped much last night. The thought of a quick dip in the lake energized her. She shed her clothes, pulling on her hiking boots and an oversized sweatshirt that hit her mid-thigh; then she stepped out of the tent and put coffee on to heat on a little propane stove she'd brought with her. She gathered the supplies she'd need to bathe and ran down to the shore. After leaving her sweatshirt and boots there, along with a big, fluffy towel, she grabbed a bar of soap from its little plastic container and plunged into the water.

The water was chillier than she anticipated. A gasp would have escaped her at the shock the temperature delivered, but the cold water seemed to suck her breath from her chest. Speed was her best bet now. In one fluid movement, she arched her body and dove into the lake. She broke the surface of the water, tossing her hair out of her face, then hurriedly soaped her skin and hair, bobbing down to rinse off the soap. From the time she left the shore to the moment she felt clean, only a few minutes had passed, but she was ready to get out of the water.

Shayla swam to the shore. When her feet touched bottom, she walked out, dropping her soap into its container; then she cocooned her hair in the towel, squeezing out as much water as she could before she wrapped the towel around her. She used her sweatshirt to dry her feet before shoving them into her hiking boots.

She rolled up the sweatshirt, picked up the soap container, and froze in place when she heard something large coming through the trees. Holding her breath, she strained to listen. To try to distinguish if the interloper was human or an animal. She was fairly certain she'd rather face a bear than deal with a two-legged brute up to no good. The thought of someone with nefarious plans catching her in her current state of undress made panic well up inside her.

With careful, quiet movements, she hastened toward her camp, trying to think of what she could use as a weapon that might inflict enough damage to let her get away. The only thing she had at hand was a mag flashlight. She grabbed it off the stump where she'd left it last night and wielded it like a club in her upraised arm as whoever, or whatever, crashed through the brush, heading straight for her. Absently, she wondered if the intruder would take her seriously if she brandished a weapon the same color as Barney the dinosaur.

Maybe it would be a better plan to call one of her friends and ask them to come to her rescue.

By the time someone drove out to where she'd parked on a little-used U.S. Forest Service road and hiked over a hill to reach her, Shayla concluded her dead body would likely be resting at the bottom of the lake.

"Get a grip, girl," Shayla muttered under her breath. Obviously, she needed to stop enjoying so many police dramas on television. Perhaps she should listen to Fynlee and Sage James at HPH and watch a few of the sweet romances on the Hallmark channel.

Shayla glanced at the tent a few yards away, gauging if she had enough time to yank on clothes before the intruder appeared. If she pretended her life depended on it, which it might, she thought she could at least get a pair of pants and a shirt pulled on, which had to be better than a damp towel.

In her haste to reach the tent with her hiking boots untied and flapping loose, she tripped over a fallen tree branch. She would have sprawled on her face if a pair of muscled arms hadn't caught her and kept her upright.

Something zinged up both arms, crossed in her brain, and traveled down to her toes, making goose bumps break out on her skin.

Her gaze traveled from the tanned, bulging bicep in front of her line of vision to a shoulder rounded with muscle, clearly defined by the crisp T-shirt the man wore. She tipped her head back and looked into a face covered by a dark scruff of whiskers. The roguish growth of hair failed to disguise his handsome features. His nose was a little too big and slightly crooked, like it had been broken at some point, but it enhanced his masculine appeal. A mole centered high on his left cheek did nothing to detract from his good looks. Her perusal took in eyes that were more gray than blue, rimmed with thick, dark lashes.

Why did guys always get the incredible eyelashes? Shayla wasn't one who wore a lot of makeup, but she felt naked without at least a few coats of mascara.

She noticed the Army logo on the front of the ball cap tilted back on his short, dark brown hair as he studied her. His expression was unreadable, as though he'd be great at playing poker, although she detected a hint of humor mingling with surprise in his stormy eyes.

He relaxed his hold on her arms, and she took an unsteady step back, letting her gaze rove over him from head to toe. Her would-be assailant looked like he bench-pressed MINI Coopers instead of weights. His T-shirt, ironed with creases on the sleeves no less, molded to his chest, highlighting his sculpted muscles. Thighs the size of small tree trunks strained against the seams of the pressed cargo pants he wore.

Shayla sucked in a breath. She had no idea who the man was or what he was doing at her campsite, but if he planned to kill her, at least she'd die looking at a beautiful creation, and she didn't mean the lake, or the woods.

"Oh, my," she whispered when he reached down and picked up the flashlight she'd dropped, handing it back to her.

His gaze tangled with hers. She decided if he'd planned to do something terrible to her, he wouldn't have placed her makeshift weapon back into her hands. Besides, there was a gentleness about him that she couldn't begin to explain, but knew, to the very depths of her being, it existed.

He might look like he could wrestle a bear and win, but she was no longer afraid of him.

Shayla straightened her awkward posture, tossed the flashlight into the tent on her sleeping bag along with her sweatshirt and soap, and boldly glared at the intruder as she tightened her grip on the towel that had dipped precariously low when she'd tripped.

"Might I inquire as to why you're standing in the middle of my camp?" she asked, trying to sound confident as the breeze blew up the back of the towel.

Rather than answer, he offered her a long, studying glance. She realized she probably looked like a throwback to cavedwellers with her hair in a snarled mess. It always looked like birds might nest in it until she combed out the tangles. Also, she likely had buffalo breath, since she hadn't yet brushed her teeth. Confidence flagging, she tried not to breathe directly on him.

He grinned and took a step back, as though he'd read her mind. Shayla glanced down and hiked the towel up, securing it tightly in her armpit.

It was just her luck to run into a hunky guy when she looked like a waterlogged cat.

"Why are you here?" she asked when he continued to stare at her. Efforts to act nonchalantly failed miserably as hysteria bubbled in her stomach and threatened to claw up her throat.

"I could ask you the same question," he finally said, hiking one dark eyebrow toward his perfectly straight hairline. "Do you realize you're trespassing on private property?"

"What? Isn't this Rockdale Lake? It's open to the public." As Shayla said the words, she realized she'd never actually seen a sign to denote the area as Rockdale Lake. In fact, the road she'd parked on had one tiny Forest Service sign out on the main road, but no others. No campground signs. Nothing.

She'd wondered why she'd never seen anyone else out at the lake the past times she'd camped there. It had seemed odd there were no public restrooms, picnic tables, or other facilities. She'd just assumed it was one of those primitive locations where nothing was provided.

Regardless, it was one of the prettiest lakes she'd ever seen. A grassy knoll stood on one end of the lake with a cabin on the other end near a babbling creek. She assumed the cabin was probably a caretaker's home, or maybe even a place for rent.

"This is not Rockdale Lake. I've never even heard of it. It's Holiday Lake, and you're on private property. I'll have to ask you to pack up and leave." He glanced around, as though expecting her to have someone there with her, but Shayla was alone. Completely alone. In retrospect, it was not the smartest move she'd made, camping off someplace no one would likely ever find her, especially since she'd thought she was somewhere else entirely.

This would be the last time she went off in the woods by herself, at least to an unknown location. The reality of how careless she'd been slammed over her. If this guy had been a serial killer or someone up to no good, she'd be dead, and no one would ever find her body.

The past three years, since she'd Googled nearby lakes, she'd been camping at this particular spot. Then again, it wasn't like she came out every weekend. More like three or four times a year.

The thought of never returning made her sad. Truly, it was one of the most picturesque places she'd ever seen. It was like it had remained untouched by humans and no one dared change it, with the exception of the cabin, dock, and footbridge.

"I'm sorry. I didn't realize I was trespassing, sir. Are you the caretaker of the property?" she asked, edging toward the tent.

"Something like that." He glanced at the coffee about to boil over. "Want me to turn that off?"

"Sure. You might as well have a cup while I get dressed." She took another step toward the tent. "You will give me time to do that much before you chase me off, won't you?"

The man offered her another long look, then nodded once. "I suppose."

The intensity of his gaze, the spark in his eye, made heat simmer in her midsection and spiral out to every extremity. Her cheeks felt like they flamed with embarrassment as she rushed into the tent and yanked on the zipper to close the flap.

Available on Amazon

Books in the Pink Pistol Sisterhood Series

In Her Sights **by Karen Witemeyer**
Book 1 ~ March 30
Love on Target **by Shanna Hatfield**
Book 2 ~ April 10
Love Under Fire **by Cheryl Pierson**
Book 3 ~ April 20
Bullet Proof Bride **by Kit Morgan**
Book 4 ~ April 30
Bullseye Bride **by Kari Trumbo**
Book 5 ~ May 10
Disarming His Heart **by Winnie Griggs**
Book 6 ~ May 20
One Shot at Love **by Linda Broday**
Book 7 ~ May 30
Armed & Marvelous **by Pam Crooks**
Book 8 ~ June 10
Lucky Shot **by Jeannie Watt**
Book 9 ~ June 20
Aiming for His Heart **by Julie Benson**
Book 10 ~ June 30
Pistol Perfect **by Jessie Gussman**
Book 11 ~ July 10

See all the Pink Pistol Sisterhood Books on the Amazon Series Page or our website.

About the Author

PHOTO BY SHANA BAILEY PHOTOGRAPHY

USA Today bestselling author Shanna Hatfield is a farm girl who loves to write. Her sweet historical and contemporary romances are filled with sarcasm, humor, hope, and hunky heroes.

When Shanna isn't dreaming up unforgettable characters, twisting plots, or covertly seeking dark, decadent chocolate, she hangs out with her beloved husband, Captain Cavedweller, at their home in the Pacific Northwest.

Shanna loves to hear from readers.
Connect with her online:
Website: shannahatfield.com
Email: shanna@shannahatfield.com